Andrew J. Brandt

CAPROCK PUBLISHING GROUP
AMARILLO TX

Caprock Publishing Group | 2207 S. Western, Suite 90, Amarillo, TX 79109

Paperback Edition January 2024

For information about bulk, educational and other special discounts, please contact Caprock Publishing Group.

CPG can bring Andrew J Brandt to your live event. For more information or to book an event, contact Caprock Publishing Group.

Cover Design: Derek Porterfield

Interior Design: Caprock Concepts

Editing: Brandon Biggers

ISBN: 9781737348702

CAPROCK PUBLISHING GROUP
AMARILLO TX

MIXTAPE FOR THE
END OF THE WORLD
A Novel

To Ellie

For everyone who has supported every crazy dream I've ever had.

To every Derrick, AJ and Dustin out there.

And to Jennifer—life with you is better than any dream.

one

At 11:59PM on December 31, 1999, the world would end. All the computers would shut down, the satellites would fall from the sky and the rich people would hole up in their bunkers until it was safe to come out. The news every day was inundated with talk of the coming aftermath of something called *Y2K*.

Derrick wondered, staring out the window from the backseat of his mother's Toyota Corolla, how it had come to this. How could the smartest minds that ever lived, who created the computers on which everything ran, have missed this one thing? It had something to do with two digits, the *19* in front of the *99*. And once it rolled over to 00, making the computers think that it was actually 1900 and not 2000, it was all over. Those lazy computer programmers, it was all their fault.

He would be witness to the end of the world, and he would do it without any of the friends he grew up with. That thought made him more sad than anything.

Ahead of them, the U-Haul driven by Doug, his mom's fiancé, took the exit from the highway and after a few more minutes, they were on Main Street of this small town that would be their new home. The wedding wasn't until the first weekend of October, but Doug and their mother had sat the kids down around the weekend of July 4th and told them the plan. She would transfer her position as bank officer to a branch in Mount Vernon.

The soon-to-be-newlyweds were much more excited about it than Derrick was, though he feigned happiness. In reality, he was just…sad. Sad to move away from home, away from everything he'd known.

Though Clearwater was a small town, it was the only place they'd ever lived. Moving to a new place in the middle of high school sounded stressful.

Cassandra was much less diplomatic with her reaction, and she ended up crying at the kitchen table, arguing that her graduation was just two years away and she wanted to graduate in Clearwater. She, too, eventually capitulated.

"We don't want to move you guys in the middle of the semester, so we are going to move to Mount Vernon the week before school starts next month," their mother had told them.

"Dee and I both think that it will help alleviate any issues in getting acclimated to the new town and the new school instead of moving you guys in October after the wedding," Doug had said.

Small towns had this uncanny ability to resemble each other, their Main Street arteries lined with buildings that housed mom-and-pops, pawn shops and hardware stores.

In fact, judging from the stores and the buildings, he could see that Mount Vernon wasn't much bigger than the town they'd left.

As they passed the line of stores and shops, one of the storefronts caught his attention. An electric guitar hung in the window that faced the street, seemingly welcoming him to this new town. For a fleeting second as Derrick saw the Corolla's pewter reflection in the store's window, he felt happiness. He made note of the shop's name, which was written in a bold red font on a chipping white sign above the door.

Sherman Music Store.

Once they were all settled into Doug's house, with their things unpacked, Derrick vowed to visit Sherman Music Store and gawk at the instruments that he'd wish he had the money for.

"This town looks stupid, mom," Cassandra whined.

Derrick and Cassandra were what some people called Irish twins, born exactly eleven months apart. They both had the same unruly hair that fell in curls, except Cassandra's was much longer and it fell over her shoulders in coiled cascades of blonde that bounced every time they hit a pothole in the street.

"It's not stupid," their mother Dee said, looking at them through the rearview mirror. "The schools here are great and you'll make new friends in no time."

"Whatever. I don't understand why we had to move here and Doug couldn't just move to Clearwater."

Derrick seconded that sentiment, though silently. He also didn't understand why the three of them had to uproot from everything they'd ever known and move three hundred miles away to this town that hugged the Red River and the Texas state line. All of their belongings, the only remnants of the home they left behind, currently resided in the box truck in front of them.

As if she could read their collective minds, Dee glanced through the mirror again. "It made more sense for us to move here because of his job. It was easier for me to transfer here as opposed to him trying to get a position with the police department there. We've gone over this time and time again, Cassandra." Her tone became more perturbed as she spoke.

Dee and Doug had met through mutual friends, and though they lived several hours apart, had started dating. Doug would come to spend the weekends with them, but this was the first time all three of them had come to this new town. Doug was the chief of the local police department. He didn't have any kids of his own and though he'd been kind and loving toward Derrick and Cassandra, Derrick still held his reservations about moving in with him.

"Well, it's still stupid," Cassandra huffed, though she stared out the window to avert their mother's stern stare.

To break up the tension, Derrick asked, "When does school start here?"

"Next week," Dee said.

"Do they have a music program?"

"They do. Doug was telling me you'll really like the music teacher, too," Dee answered. She gave him a smile. "Look, guys," she said as they turned onto a residential street, "this is going to be a learning experience for all three of us. Doug loves both of you like you're his own. Just be patient and courteous."

The houses that lined the street looked like mansions compared to the three-bedroom-one-bathroom home they left behind in Clearwater. Large archways and covered porticos ringed the two-story brick homes. Even Cassandra's attitude changed when she saw the homes.

"This is where we're going to live?" she said, her jaw wide open.

"Yes it is. I told you that you guys would like it here," Dee said with a happy grin.

Derrick stared at it all. The houses looked huge, but he was homesick already for Clearwater. He knew where everything was back home. He knew that it was only six blocks from the house to the convenience store where he'd buy a Mountain Dew and then another four blocks to the library or five blocks to RadioShack. This new town was so foreign and he already felt claustrophobic.

Ahead of them, the U-Haul pulled into the driveway of one of the houses. Two stories like many of the rest, it was a light yellow brick home with a large front yard immaculately trimmed and green. Dee pulled the Corolla in behind the U-Haul as Doug backed the truck up to the garage doors.

Dee parked the car and they all got out as Doug hopped out of the large truck and stretched. "Man, that thing is a beating to drive," he said. He was tall and lanky, but with wide shoulders. When he smiled, his top lip disappeared beneath his salt-and-pepper mustache. Dee gave him a large hug, the top of her head with her blonde hair tied in a bun barely reaching the top of his chest. Embracing her, Doug told them all, "Welcome to your new home. I hope you like it."

Derrick looked around at the surrounding homes on the block. Across the street, a large white cottage-style home housed a Range Rover in the circular driveway in front. It was much nicer than anything back in Clearwater. The houses here looked like something doctors and attorneys would live in and it felt so much different from their neighborhood he'd grown up in.

Cassandra blurted out, "Wow! These houses are so nice!"

Doug chuckled. "This is one of the older neighborhoods here in Mount Vernon, back when they built this style. Why don't we go inside for a Dr. Pepper before we start unloading it all? I'll show you your bedrooms."

Cassandra beamed and looked at Derrick. "Come on," she said excitedly. "Let's go in!"

She walked ahead of him, her frizzy hair bouncing on her shoulders as she did. Doug opened the garage door from the panel mounted beside it.

"If you guys need to go in through here, the code is my birthday, 1113," he said as the mechanism roared to life and the door lifted. Inside the garage sat a Toyota Tacoma pickup and a black motorcycle.

Derrick's eyes went straight to the motorcycle.

"No, sir," Dee said, probably sensing his widened gaze at the Honda Rebel. "Don't even think about it."

"It's a beginner's bike," Doug chimed in. "It would be good for you to learn on, but definitely with supervision."

Dee shot him a look and Doug shrugged his shoulders. "What? I was riding motorcycles when I was his age."

Dee shook her head and as she walked into the house from the garage, Doug turned to Derrick. "She's the queen of this castle now, so we have to do what she says."

Derrick smiled and agreed. He liked Doug well enough. He was always kind to them when he'd come to Clearwater to spend time with them, but he knew that it would be different with them all living together now.

Doug held the door open and Derrick stepped in under the man's arm and looked around. It was huge, and open. Doug had obviously spent some time making sure the place was spotless and clean, something Derrick knew would impress his mom. She always kept their home back in Clearwater immaculate, even if his own bedroom constantly looked like a laundry bomb had gone off.

"This is it," Doug announced. "Pantry is over there, fridge and stove, of course. The living room is here," he pointed to the room with a large leather sectional that sat in front of an enormous Pioneer television. The screen was huge, at least five feet wide and it sat on a pedestal that housed the speakers.

"That is the biggest television I have ever seen!" Cassandra exclaimed.

"Yup, and I've got a PlayStation and a Nintendo 64 hooked up to it," Doug said, much to the excitement of both Derrick and Cassandra. Derrick couldn't wait to play *Tony Hawk* on that giant screen.

"Which we will only play after homework is done," Dee said.

Cassandra whined again. "Oh come on, mom! School doesn't start til next week!"

"Right," Dee said. "Which means we only have a week to get you registered and make sure the curriculum here matches what you guys had in Clearwater."

Cassandra groaned. Derrick just stared at it all. Above the mantle in the living room, a picture of Doug sat in a dusty frame. He was much younger in the picture, wearing a uniform. Mounted to the frame was a gold nameplate that read Douglas J. Reynolds, Academy Class 1992. He'd only been a police officer for seven years, which made Derrick wonder how he became Chief so quickly or so young. Back in Clearwater, the chief of police was always an old gray-haired man with a burly mustache. It seemed strange. Beside the academy photo, there were other pictures too, and Derrick saw that he had one of Dee and the kids already up there.

"Come on, I'll show you the bedrooms," Doug said.

He led them through a long hallway. "The master suite is upstairs, which means you two will get plenty of privacy down here," he said over his shoulder.

"This one is yours, Cassandra," he said, opening the door. Inside, the walls were painted a light yellow. It was large and open, with plenty of room for her vanity and dresser.

She squealed with excitement. "This is great!" she said.

Doug laughed. "There's a jack-and-jill bathroom between the two rooms, and you each have your own sink. And then," he opened the door to the second bedroom at the end of the hall. Doug grinned at Derrick. "This one is yours."

Inside, the room was a plain white square with beige carpet.

But in the middle of the room, sitting on a foldable black guitar rack, was a red Fender Telecaster.

two

♫ PEARL JAM - EVEN FLOW ♫

"Doug!" Dee said. "That's too much!"

Derrick was speechless. He looked up at Doug, almost as if to ask *Is that mine?*

Doug just shrugged again. "Look, I wanted you guys to know that this is your home too. So, I figured a house-warming gift was in order."

Dee turned to Derrick, "Well?" she implored. "What do you say?"

"Thank you so much," he said. But Derrick was still in shock. He'd never had a brand-new guitar before. In the back of the U-Haul, his old Epiphone acoustic guitar was packed in its case. He couldn't wait to get everything unpacked and play the new electric guitar.

He'd always liked Telecasters and would often go to the Terry's Music in Clearwater to play them whenever he could. He'd daydream about being able to go in one day and purchase one for himself.

"Alright, let's get to work," Dee said. Derrick and

Cassandra followed their mom and Doug back outside. On the way out, Doug stopped at the refrigerator in the garage and withdrew a handful of maroon soda cans, tossing one to each of them. They cracked them open, and Derrick drank his greedily. It tasted so good and felt so cold in his throat on the hot summer day.

"We'll get everything out and into the garage first so we don't have to work all day in the sun," Doug said.

He unclasped the latch on the back of the U-Haul truck and threw it open. Hopping onto the deck, he started pulling out boxes, sliding them to the ledge, where Derrick and Cassandra would pull them down and place them in the garage. They left behind or sold all the large appliances back in Clearwater, so mostly they just packed their personal belongings. Aside from their beds, the mattresses stacked on their sides toward the back of the truck, the only large pieces of furniture were Cassandra's vanity and Derrick's large five-drawer dresser.

Doug heaved a box from the truck. "Goodness," he said, wiping his brow. "What's in all these?"

"Clothes, mostly," Cassandra said, pulling the box down and sliding it across the concrete of the garage floor.

Grabbing a box himself and sliding it into the garage, Derrick knew that was the truth. Cassandra had more clothes than anyone Derrick had ever known, even after donating two bags' worth before leaving Clearwater.

They worked like this over the course of the next hour and a half, stopping occasionally for a breather before finally getting the entire truck unloaded. Once they had all the boxes in the garage, Derrick and Cassandra were responsible for the boxes labelled with their names, tasked with taking them to their bedrooms to begin unboxing it all. Doug and Dee came in behind them, building the beds on their rails and putting the headboards in place.

Derrick found his Walkman and pulled the headphones over his ears. He pushed play and Eddie Vedder's voice filled his head. He let the music flood over him. The tape, a mixtape that was a parting gift from his friend Jerod back in Clearwater, was full of their favorite bands, including several songs off of Pearl Jam's album Ten. They had both discovered music over the last year, finding solace in grunge bands like Pearl Jam and Fuel.

By the time Derrick had all his belongings unpacked, he'd played through both sides of the tape. The room looked nice, if sterile. He'd take time to hang a few posters and make it more a reflection of himself, but for now he couldn't wait to get his hands on that new guitar that called his name from the corner. He'd set his acoustic beside it, the instruments a makeshift shrine to his burgeoning passion.

With the headphones still on his ears, he picked up the red Telecaster, feeling the weight of the instrument. The body, a solid block of ash with a maple fretboard and neck, was heavier than he'd anticipated. The back was a flat slab of wood with holes where the strings were anchored. He sat on the edge of his bed and strummed a few chords along with the Pearl Jam tape that he'd flipped back to Side A. He never noticed Doug standing in the open doorway, leaning against the frame, his arms crossed over his chest.

Derrick looked up and pulled the headphones off his ears, letting them hang around his neck.

"What do you think?" Doug asked.

"It's really cool. I've never had an electric guitar before."

"I know," Doug said. "I thought it would help ease the transition. Plus, the Fender Telecaster is the ultimate rock-star guitar. Springsteen, Richards, both play this guitar. Dee thought it was excessive, but, hey, what kid doesn't want an electric guitar? I hope you don't mind. I didn't know what to get Cassandra, so I gave her money to buy some new clothes at the mall."

"Yeah," Derrick said. "That's probably the best thing you could get her, honestly." A smile crept across his face, and for the first time all day he felt relaxed, like things would be okay. "This guitar is really great. Thank you so much. I'm just," he trailed off. Then, "I'm just not used to having nice things like this."

"I wanted to get you something to help you feel welcomed," Doug said. He nodded to the headphones looped around Derrick's neck. "What are you listening to?"

"Oh, just a mixtape. Pearl Jam and stuff." He showed Doug the cassette's handwritten label which Jerod had scrawled the names of the bands and songs on it in Sharpie.

"Oh yeah?" Doug's eyebrows perked up. "When I was in Saudi Arabia, I had some buddies that were all into that Seattle grunge stuff, probably a year before Nirvana got really huge. A guy gave me a tape from a band called Mother Love Bone. Their guitarist went on to form Pearl Jam with Eddie Vedder and the rest of the guys."

"Really?" Derrick asked. To him, Doug always seemed more like a Garth Brooks or George Strait kind of guy, a country-loving lawman.

"Yes sir. I was all into those bands, especially after I got back to the States and entered the police academy. We would copy tapes for each other, just like this. All this stuff coming out of Seattle during the big grunge explosion. Soundgarden, Mudhoney, all those guys. I might still have some of them, actually." Doug chewed on the inside of his cheek for a moment. "I think they're in a box in the attic space above the garage. Tomorrow, I'll climb up there, see if I can find them."

"That would be cool," Derrick said.

"Well, listen, I hope you guys get settled in. I know moving is hard and can be scary, getting used to a new place," Doug said. "I've been all over, and if there's one piece of advice I can give, it would be to find people who make you feel at home. Know what I mean?"

"Yeah, I think so." As they talked, Derrick could hear the tape begin to warble. He looked down at the Walkman clipped to his waistband of his jeans. The battery indicator was flashing. "Oh no," he said. "Batteries are going dead."

"I think I have some double-A's in the kitchen drawer," Doug pointed a thumb down the hall.

"No, I have some in my backpack. I left it out in mom's car though," Derrick said.

"Alright, well, shut the garage door when you're done. It's the button by the door."

"I will," Derrick nodded.

"I'm heading upstairs to help your mom finish unpacking. If you need anything else, let me know. I hope you like it here. We'll get to know each other really well."

Derrick nodded again, and Doug went down one end of

the hall to the stairs that led up to the master suite, and Derrick headed through the kitchen and into the garage. He pulled the backdoor of the Corolla open and found his backpack, the canvas bag still warm from being in the car all evening. Checking the top pocket to make sure the package of batteries was still in there, he slung it over his shoulder and started back into the garage.

A single-cab pickup truck, its blue paint looking almost black in the darkness, pulled up to the curb of the house next door and Derrick glanced over and stopped in his tracks.

The pickup's passenger door opened and a girl stepped out. She looked to be his age, but was more gorgeous than any person he'd ever seen in his life. Even in the glow of the streetlamp lights that lined the street, she was captivating. Long brown hair fell down her shoulders and, with a slender frame, she glided more than she actually walked. The truck roared off, its muffler breaking the silence of the moment.

The girl started walking up the pathway to her front door and looked over at Derrick, standing in the light of the open garage, backpack slung haphazardly over one shoulder, threatening to slide off.

"Hi," she said.

Derrick, his whole body going tense with teenage nervousness, quickly waved and went inside, hitting the garage door button harder than he'd meant to.

three

♫ GOO GOO DOLLS - FALLIN' DOWN ♫

THE ENTIRETY OF THE NEXT WEEK WAS A LONELY BLUR OF school registration, class scheduling and shopping for supplies. Derrick wondered what that first day would be like, starting sophomore year in a new place. Despite being a grade apart, both he and Cassandra had the same history class—World History—since their previous school taught the history classes in a different order.

On the morning of that first day, Derrick got dressed, pulling on a pair of jeans, his black Chuck Taylors and a black t-shirt emblazoned with the CBGB logo across the front. He'd never been to New York, never even been to a punk rock concert before, but he'd once seen the lead singer of the Third Eye Blind wearing the exact same shirt. He found one at the mall in Clearwater back at the beginning of summer and snatched it up almost immediately.

Going into the kitchen, he found Cassandra sitting at the kitchen bar in one of the stools that resided at it. Though Doug's house—their house, he had to remind himself, though it still didn't quite feel like home—had a formal dining room, they ate most of their meals together at the bar in the kitchen. Cassandra was working on a bowl of cereal when Derrick walked in. Her hair, normally frizzy and curled, was straightened, falling well below her shoulder blades. She wore a skirt that barely went to her knees. Turning to see him as he shuffled in, she gave him a once over.

"You look like a slob," she said.

"Well, you look like a prep," he retorted.

Cassandra scoffed as she shoved a spoonful of Froot Loops in her mouth. Dee came down from upstairs, followed by Doug in his police uniform.

"Good morning," Dee said. She looked at Derrick. "That's what you're wearing on the first day?" she asked, giving him a judgmental up-and-down.

Derrick shrugged. "This is what I like."

"I just thought you'd want to make a good first impression," his mother said.

Doug clapped him on the shoulder. "Leave the boy alone. You want him to go to school on the first day looking like Urkel?"

"Well, no," Dee argued. "But I don't want him looking like Kurt Cobain either."

Derrick feigned mourning. "May he rest in peace," he muttered.

Cassandra scoffed again. "God, he's been dead since we were in kindergarten."

"It's only been five years, Cass," Derrick said as he shot her a look of disdain. "I know you were in kindergarten five years ago, but only because you had to repeat it a half dozen times."

"Whatever," Cassandra said. "Anyway, don't talk to me today. I don't want you to ruin my first day by people knowing we're related."

"Cassandra Nicole," Dee said as she poured a cup of coffee after pulling a mug from the counter. "That's not nice."

"I'm not trying to be nice, mom," she said. "I'm trying to make new friends."

"I don't want people thinking I'm the brother of some snobby prep like you anyway," Derrick said.

"That's enough," Dee said, her hands on her hips. "Both of you."

Doug chuckled to himself as he held out his travel mug for Dee to fill from the glass carafe. He kissed her. "Alright. I'll see you guys this evening," he said. "Enjoy your first day. And please, don't give your mom a hard time."

"We won't," both Derrick and Cassandra said, almost in unison.

"I won't be home until close to seven," Doug said as he sipped his coffee. "What kind of pizza do you guys want? I'll stop by Pizza Point on my way home."

"Do they have deep dish?" Derrick asked.

"They make a great Chicago-style pie," Doug said. "That sounds really good."

Dee and Cassandra both requested a supreme pizza, full of mushrooms, peppers and Italian sausage. Derrick preferred his pizza simple—pepperoni and cheese.

Doug kissed his fiancé again and left through the garage

door. Cassandra went back to her cereal as Derrick poured himself a bowl from the box. He poured in enough milk until the bowl nearly overflowed with pastel rings of sugar.

"We need to leave in about 15 minutes," Dee said.

"I think I'm going to walk," Derrick said.

Dee raised an eyebrow. "Are you sure? You don't want to be seen with mom on the first day?"

Derrick mumbled a "No, I think I'll be fine" with a mouthful of cereal.

"God, Derrick. Don't talk with your mouth full. It's rude," Cassandra hissed.

In response, he rolled his eyes and shoved another spoon of cereal into his mouth, chomping loudly.

Dee snapped her fingers. "What did I say? Be nice." The last two words were sharp and succinct.

After finishing his breakfast, Derrick grabbed his backpack and Walkman from his bedroom, kissed his mom goodbye and started down the road. As he walked on the sidewalk, he glanced at the house next door, the one where the girl that he'd seen the night they moved in lived. He'd seen her in passing a couple of times since, every time stopping in his tracks. He had no idea what her name was or anything else about her other than that she lived next door and she was the most beautiful girl he'd ever seen. He hoped that, as he walked past, she would come out from the front door at the same time. In his imagination, he thought about walking to school together.

"Oh hey," he would say. "You walk to school too?"

"I do," she would answer. "What grade are you in?"

"I'm a sophomore."

"No way! Me too!"

They would walk side-by-side and he would fall in love with every word she spoke.

However, it didn't happen. He walked by, the front door held shut, not seeing the girl next door. After he passed her house, he pulled his headphones over his shaggy blonde hair and pushed play on the Walkman. He had put in a tape that Doug had found in the attic. It was from a band called Goo Goo Dolls. Derrick had heard a couple of their songs, but Doug explained that before they were mainstream, they were a punk band from Buffalo, and that he should give the tape a listen. So, he shoved it in the device before walking out the door and let the sounds drown out his anxiety and first-day jitters. He found himself bobbing his head to the music. It was raw and edgy. He couldn't believe this was Doug's at one time.

The walk to school was an uneventful eight blocks. As he got closer to the campus, he saw more cars, could hear the cacophony of music blaring from vehicle sound systems in the high school's parking lot.

The sprawling campus looked huge, from the main building, to the gym and football field. As he got closer, Derrick pulled his class schedule from his back pocket to determine which door to go through. The first class listed was Biology I, in room 1102. His mother had brought both him and Cassandra to the school earlier that week to see where their classes were, but now he wished he'd spent more time paying attention to the exact location of each classroom. He hadn't even made it to the front doors of the school and he already felt lost.

In front of the school, sandwiched between the front entrance and a large horseshoe drive through, was a collection of round concrete tables and benches. There were several groups of students congregated there, all different stereotypical cliques. It didn't matter which school or which city you were in, the group dynamics remained static. A huddle of boys in athletic shorts and letter jackets—despite the temperature climbing close to eighty degrees in the afternoons—stood together while another group of boys in baggy jeans and beanies played hacky sack in a circle nearby.

There was a group of girls huddled together, backpacks slung over their shoulders. Though Derrick scanned their faces for the girl next door, she was nowhere to be seen.

Derrick didn't know where to go. He knew he would stick out like a sore thumb sitting by himself on one of those concrete tables, but he didn't know how to approach any of the kids to introduce himself. Before he could, the bell rang, a sharp, high-pitched chime breaking through the sound of music in his headphones. He fell in order behind the rest of the students as they all started making their way into the halls of the school.

Fluorescent lights above them shone brightly, reflecting off the speckled linoleum floor. The lockers lining the hallway, all in Mount Vernon maroon and white, were rushed upon as students began depositing their backpacks and pulling supplies for their first classes.

Derrick looked again at his class schedule and decided to try to spend the next four minutes looking for the classroom. He'd find his locker later.

"1102," he said aloud to himself. An open door close by had a black plaque with white lettering mounted next to it. It read 1120, which meant he should be able to find 1102 at the end of this long hall.

Shouldering his way down the hallway, Derrick followed the plaques mounted beside each door until he got to 1102. He stood in front of the door and stared at it, confused.

It was the supply closet.

He looked down at his schedule again to verify that he'd read it correctly then looked back up at the sign on the wall beside the door: **1102 SUPPLIES**

"Are you lost?"

The girl's voice came from beside him and, pulling his headphones off his ears, he turned to the source.

It was *her*.

The neighbor girl.

She wore a pair of jeans that flared at the bottom and a blue spaghetti strap shirt covered by a denim jacket. A black choker necklace fit snugly around her neck. She looked gorgeous, with her brown hair framing her round face and falling over her shoulders.

"Uh…" he stammered. "I, uh…" He stopped to collect his words.

"What class are you looking for?" she asked.

He simply handed her the paper schedule in his hands.

"Oh, Coach Vargas," she said. "The front office must have mistyped this. He's in 1120, at the other end of the hall."

Derrick sighed. *Of course it was.*

She looked at the schedule again. "D. Townsend. What's the 'D' stand for?"

Derrick took the schedule as she handed it back to him. "I'm Derrick," he finally was able to get out.

"I'm Haley," she said. "I'll walk with you to class." She started down the hall back toward 1120 and Derrick fell in step beside her.

Haley. She had a name, and it was Haley.

"Didn't you guys move in next door to me last week?" she asked as they walked.

"Yeah," he said.

"I thought so. You looked familiar. Is Chief Davis your dad?"

"My stepdad. Well, about to be. My mom and him are getting married in October and they decided it was best that we move in before school started," Derrick said.

"That's cool," she said. "He's been our neighbor for a long time. Well, ever since the old Chief died."

Derrick's brows furrowed. "The Chief inherits the house of the old one?"

She laughed. "No. His dad was the old chief. And then when he died, the new Chief Davis got the job, and he also inherited the house. My dad is on the city council so they talk a lot."

"Oh, cool," Derrick said. That explained why Doug had the job while being so young. Small-town politics.

"Yeah," Haley said. "We always have a back-to-school pool party in my backyard the weekend after school starts. It'll be this Saturday. You should come over. Since we're neighbors. You'll be able to meet everyone here at school better that way."

"Oh, um," Derrick stammered again, mentally kicking

himself in the ass. He felt like he looked stupid, unable to get words out of his mouth. He always imagined he'd have more confidence when it came to girls, but anytime a member of the fairer sex talked to him, he clammed up for some unexplainable reason. Perhaps it was because now all he could think about was this gorgeous girl in a bikini. "Yeah, that sounds great."

The tardy bell rang just as they walked into class and as Haley took a seat next to her friends who waved her over, Derrick took the only free seat left, toward the front of the classroom. As he sat down, he glanced back at Haley and she gave him a wave. It filled him with a nervous warmth.

Coach Vargas, a short, squat man with tan arms and sunburned nose under a visor, black hair spilling out the top, came into the classroom and sat a shoulder bag onto the desk. He introduced himself to the class, though it was apparent that he was well-known in the school. As he took the roll, he got to Derrick's name. "Townsend?" he said.

Derrick raised his hand.

"You a new student?" the coach asked.

"Yes sir."

"Great. Where are you from?"

"Clearwater, sir," Derrick said sheepishly.

"Well, welcome to Mount Vernon High. Hope you like it here," he said.

Derrick mouthed a *thank you* and Coach Vargas got to the work of the day which amounted to nothing more than going over classroom and lab rules and the syllabus for the semester. Each student received a packet with classroom requirements, including lab tools. Derrick flipped through the syllabus and saw that they'd be dissecting frogs later in the semester.

After the bell rang and class was dismissed for their next period, Coach Vargas stopped Derrick on his way out the door. "I know coming to a new school can be rough and making new friends isn't easy, but getting involved in extracurricular activities can help. Do you play any sports?"

Derrick said no, but that he was signed up for choir and theater.

"Try tennis out. I've been coaching for twenty years, and we've been to State every year for the past decade. It's fun and we have a good time. Plus, colleges love to give out tennis scholarships."

From behind them, Haley, her arms full of books spoke up. "You should definitely try out!" she exclaimed. "We have a ton of fun. Coach Vargas is the best."

"Um, okay," Derrick replied.

"Alright, you two better get on before you're late for your next class. Where are you headed?" the coach asked.

Derrick looked at his schedule, the lines in the paper now permanent from folding and unfolding, the edges frayed from being shoved in his back pocket.

"English, with Mrs. Rogers," he said.

"Oh great, you'll love Becky. She's a great teacher. Her class is in the next wing over," Coach Vargas said.

Derrick thanked him for the advice and hurried on to the next class before the next bell rang.

In the hallway leaving Coach Vargas's classroom, Haley turned to the other direction, but not before stopping. "I'm headed to Algebra," she said. "Find me at lunch, if I don't see you before then. I'll introduce you to all my friends."

Derrick nodded and turned toward the direction of his next class with a huge grin on his face. He'd never been one to receive female attention before. In Clearwater, he was just Derrick Townsend. But, here? In this new school? He could be anyone. He liked that idea. He could be whoever he wanted to be. He could be popular. That would infuriate Cassandra, and he smiled to himself at the idea. If at this new school he was one of the popular crowd while she had to watch from the sidelines? She would really hate him then.

He arrived at Mrs. Rogers's classroom and found an anonymous seat in the middle of the rows. Right when the tardy bell rang, another student plopped into the desk next to him. Derrick looked over and did a double-take.

The kid, with a mop of brown hair that fell over his ears and nearly in his eyes, wore a pair of ripped jeans and a plaid flannel shirt tied around his waist, like an Eddie Vedder clone. And he wore the same CBGB shirt.

four

THE KID LOOKED OVER AT DERRICK AND GAVE HIM A facetious grin. "Nice shirt," he said.

"Uh, thanks," he said. "You too."

Suddenly, Derrick didn't feel so original, like an outsider to pop culture. At the same time, he felt an instant kinship with this grunge holdout.

"I'm AJ," the kid said.

"Derrick."

"You new?" AJ asked.

"Yeah. Moved here last week," Derrick said.

"Dude that sucks. I'm sorry."

"What? Why?"

Before AJ could answer the question, Mrs. Rogers, a short, plump blonde woman, shushed the class and started taking roll. When she got to AJ, calling out "Tooley, Anthony John," she looked up and saw the next kid on the list—"Townsend, Derrick"—dressed nearly identically to AJ and she gave a grin. "Did you two coordinate outfits?"

The rest of the class, not having noticed, turned their attention to the two boys in desks in the middle of the classroom and laughed as well. Derrick felt his cheeks go flush and he sunk into his desk, his back forming to the curve of the plastic seatback.

Mrs. Rogers hushed the class again and began going over their syllabus for the semester. Derrick, without turning his head, returned his attention to AJ Tooley and the kid gave him a shrug.

"Welcome to Mount Vernon," he whispered.

♪ ♪ ♪

AFTER HIS FOUR MORNING CLASSES, DERRICK FOUND HIS WAY to the cafeteria for lunch. After grabbing a brown plastic tray from a pile at the beginning of the lunch line, he made his way through the selections, pulling a slice of pizza, a basket of crinkle-cut french fries, an apple and a paper carton of chocolate milk onto the tray. Once in the open maw of the cafeteria, he scanned the room. Out of the corner of his eye, he saw Haley waving in his direction from a table surrounded by other kids.

Derrick made his way over and Haley scooted over on the bench. "Guys," she said. "This is Derrick. He just moved in next door to me. Chief Davis is his stepdad."

The group at the table, seven in all, welcomed Derrick, though he stuck out like a sore thumb in his baggy jeans and CBGB shirt. The rest of them wore Tommy Hilfiger or Chaps branded clothing.

One girl, with jet black hair and mocha skin, introduced

herself. Her name was Makenna and she asked him where he'd moved from.

"I've got a cousin that lives in Clearwater," an Asian boy said. "Do you know Tommy Tran?"

"I do," Derrick said. All these questions, coming from different people, he could hardly keep up with who was asking what. He felt like a science experiment, or a new toy. "He's a Senior this year, I think."

The Asian boy nodded. "Man, small world," he said and Derrick agreed.

Haley spoke up, "Coach Vargas asked Derrick to try out for the tennis team."

"Oh, you'd like that," the girl with the mocha skin said. "We have a lot of fun at tournaments. Have you played before?"

"No, not at all. We didn't have tennis in Clearwater."

"Well," Haley said. "Come over after school and we can go to Paramount Park and I'll teach you before you meet with Coach Vargas."

Derrick really liked the idea of spending time with Haley, so he agreed.

They all continued to eat their lunch and talk, with Derrick being the main subject of conversation. He'd never had so much attention back home in Clearwater, but he was enjoying it. Haley and her friends made him feel at ease and that perhaps this transition would be easier than he'd originally thought.

♪ ♪ ♪

THE REST OF THE DAY WENT BY QUICKLY, AND EACH CLASS WAS more or less a repeat of the previous—the teacher took roll call and went over classroom rules and the syllabus. He finally saw Cassandra in their World History class after lunch. Before the tardy bell rang, he asked her if she liked the school, and she said she did. She'd gone to lunch off campus with some kids she'd met in her Chemistry class. Juniors and Seniors were allowed to leave campus for lunch, and she'd gone to an apparently popular place called the Burger Barn, because that's where a large contingent of the upperclassmen went for their forty minutes. Derrick was jealous that she got to eat off-campus, but he told her that he'd made friends and was invited to try out for the tennis team. She scoffed at that.

"You? Tennis?" she said.

"What?" he said defensively. "It sounds like fun. Besides, I want to start over new here. Not like Clearwater. I was a nobody there."

"Well, good luck," she said.

Their conversation was cut short by the teacher, and they left in opposite directions. He hoped that her first day was going well, though. If anything, they had this kindred experience of being the new kids.

With the final bell of the day, all the students poured out of the school and into either the parking lot that resided on the east side of the campus or onto the sprawling front courtyard. Derrick started walking home when he heard a voice calling out behind him on the sidewalk.

"Hey! New kid!"

Derrick turned and saw AJ coming up the sidewalk.

After a couple seconds of half-running, he caught up to Derrick. "Hey man," AJ said. "How was your first day as a Mount Vernon Lion?"

"It was pretty cool," Derrick said. They fell in lockstep as they crossed the street. "Do you live near here?"

"Yeah, over on Orchard," AJ said.

"I don't know where that is," Derrick said. "We live on Tangerine. Tangerine and Sixteenth."

"Okay, cool. You're, like, two blocks from me then." He pointed to Derrick's headphones around his neck. "What are you listening to?"

"Just a tape that my mom's fiancé gave me." He looked down at his Walkman through the display hole. "Goo Goo Dolls. *Superstar Car Wash*. It's pretty good. Here." He pulled the headphones from around his neck and handed them to AJ.

AJ put them on as Derrick hit play and he started bobbing his head. "Dude, this is rad. I like this!"

Derrick smiled and agreed.

"What else do you listen to?" AJ asked.

Derrick answered with a list of bands that were constant residents of his Walkman's tray, including Pearl Jam, Fuel, Eve 6 and Bush.

"Dude, yes. Fuel is amazing. And Eddie Vedder is a god."

Derrick smiled and agreed.

They walked together along the sidewalks away from the school. "Where did you move from?" AJ asked.

"Clearwater."

"Whoa. What brought you all the way here?"

Derrick explained the situation of moving to Mount

Vernon, of his mom and Doug's upcoming wedding and everything else. For the first time since moving here, he felt relaxed. He felt like he had someone he could talk to. Someone like him.

They talked about music and bands until they got to Sixteenth Avenue, and Derrick pointed off in the direction of Tangerine Drive. "I'm this way."

"Cool, man. I guess I'll see you tomorrow," AJ said as he turned to cross the street.

As Derrick started walking off toward Tangerine, AJ called out. "Hey. Do you walk in the mornings too?"

"Yeah." Derrick said.

"Cool. I'll meet you here tomorrow. 7:45?"

"Sounds good man," Derrick said and tipped his hand in the air. He turned back around, pulled his headphones over his ears and pushed play.

THE TENNIS BALL CAME AT HIM AND DERRICK SWUNG THE racquet but missed. Instead, the ball clanged against the chain-link fence behind him, bounced back and rolled a few feet on the clay surface.

Breathless and sweating, he grabbed the ball from the court and called out to Haley, "How about a rest?"

He was at home when she had knocked on the front door, wearing a pair of athletic shorts and a Mount Vernon High tank top, with two racquets in hand. His mom and Cassandra practically pushed him out the door. Even on the walk to Paramount Park, a neighborhood park that stretched three blocks with a pair of tennis courts on one end, Derrick was already thinking about the ribbing he'd get when he returned home.

Haley went to the side of the court by the net and, sitting on the ground and leaning against the chain-link, took a sip from a Gatorade water bottle. Derrick sat next to her, careful not to sit too close, despite wanting to be as close to her as possible. Even with a band of sweat beading in her brow, she was the most beautiful girl he'd ever seen. He wanted to look at nothing else but her.

"You're getting the hang of it out there. You tend to tuck your elbow when you swing forehand, and that makes you swing under the ball. I'll show you how to extend your forehand swing after we take a break," she said.

"Yeah, that sounds good." Of course, she could have told him that they'd be setting his feet on fire while pelting him with tennis balls fired from a bazooka and it would still sound good coming out of her mouth.

"Did you enjoy your first day at MV?"

"Yeah. It was a lot less scary than I thought it would be. I've never been the new kid before, you know?" he said as he took a drink from his own water bottle. His mom had handed it to him as he walked out the door. "Are you from here?"

"Born and raised. My parents were high school sweethearts. Dad runs the monument company and he's on the city council. My mom stays at home, but she works at the church a couple of mornings a week. Like, babysitting little kids so other moms can run errands."

"What's a monument company?" Derrick asked.

"You know, like headstones?"

"Like at a cemetery?"

"Yeah. He designs those and cuts the granite. Well, I guess *he* doesn't cut the granite. He hires people that do that. In fact, I don't even think he designs them either to be honest." She seemed so comfortable with the idea though the thought of making gravestones gave Derrick a shiver.

Seemingly noticing Derrick's response, she gave him a quizzical look, her eyebrows furrowed and lips pursed. "What? It's not that creepy, stop making that face." She gave him a playful shove and he bounced against it. Derrick liked her, but he was also happy to know that she seemed to enjoy being around him too.

"How does someone get in the graveyard business?" Derrick asked.

"It's the monument business, thank you," she answered sarcastically. "I don't know the specifics. It's what my family has always done. My grandfather started the business back in the sixties. My dad and his brother started working there when they were teenagers. Who knows? Maybe I'll take it over when I'm old enough."

"Sounds like you have your life planned out already," Derrick said. He thought he did, too, until they were forced to move to Mt. Vernon. However, that wasn't necessarily a bad thing since he met Haley.

"I don't know about that," she said. "I don't know. What do you want to be when you grow up?"

"I want to be a rockstar," he said. "I want to make it, somehow. Record an album and play concerts all over the world."

"That's ambitious," she said. "What do you play?"

"Guitar, mostly," he said. "And some piano."

"I hated piano when I was a kid," she said. "My parents made me take lessons and it was awful. I had to learn these classical pieces that I had no interest in and then play them at recitals. I hated it. All those eyes on you, watching and listening, and you just hoping you wouldn't mess up." She took a drink of water. "I don't even remember any of those songs now."

"I started learning guitar last year."

"What do you like to listen to?" she asked.

He answered with the same list of bands he'd given AJ earlier that day.

"That's cool, I guess," she said. "I listen to N'SYNC, Britney Spears, stuff like that. I like the dancing."

Derrick didn't want to tell her that he hated those boy bands and the cookie-cutter pop music, but his judgement was apparently plastered on his face.

"Oh, so you're gonna judge me for gravestones and my taste in music? Wow." Her tone was playful, almost flirtatious.

Derrick just grinned and shrugged. "No judgement here. But I'm going to have to make you some mixtapes, help broaden your musical tastes."

"I think I would like that. Did you make any new friends today?"

"I think so," he said. "You, of course. And a couple of other guys in choir. And then this kid, AJ. He wore the same t-shirt that I did." He noticed that her face went blank, her eyes wide, when he mentioned AJ's name. "What?" he asked. "What's wrong?"

"Well, look, I'm not going to tell you who you can or can't be friends with. I mean, he's never been weird to me or anything, but..." she trailed off.

"What?" Derrick asked. "What is it?"

"I don't know. It's just a rumor, but I don't want it to affect you."

"Well, tell me," he said, turning toward her.

"Okay, but just, don't, like, be weird about it or anything. I don't even know that it's true."

Derrick's heart was racing. *What could be so bad?*

"It's just, a lot of people say that he's gay," Haley finally said.

"Really?" Derrick asked, bemused at the idea. "I didn't pick up on that at all." But then, he thought about it, the way AJ had run up to him after school, inviting him to walk to school together in the morning. That didn't necessarily mean that he was gay, though.

"Like I said, it's just a rumor. And I'm not saying that people would say the same thing about you, but I just don't want to give anyone a reason to label you or start rumors about you like that too. You just moved here," she said.

"Well, I'm definitely not gay," he said. He wanted to say, because I have a huge crush on you, but he kept the thought to himself.

"Good," Haley said.

Derrick thought about that one-word answer, hung on it. Did that mean that she was glad that he was into girls? Into her? Before he could think about it too hard, she stood up.

"Alright," Haley said, holding her hand out. Derrick took it in his own and she heaved him up on his feet. "Let's go over that forehand swing before we call it a night."

♪ ♪ ♪

DERRICK GOT HOME, WALKED UP THE STAIRS OF THE ELEVATED porch when Doug pulled up at the same time. His tie loose around his neck and the top button undone on his shirt, he looked like he'd had a long day. He balanced a couple of pizza boxes on one hand.

"Do you need help?" Derrick asked.

"Hey, kid," he said, coming from the car. ""There's a twelve pack of Dr. Pepper in the front seat if you can grab that. How was your day of school?"

"It was pretty good," Derrick said.

Behind them, Dee had the door open already. "He just got back from the tennis courts with a young lady from school," she said.

Derrick's cheeks went flush and he mumbled something about it not being a big deal. "She's teaching me how to play tennis so I can try out for the team," he said, his head low to hide his embarrassment.

Doug's eyes lit up and he squeezed Derrick's shoulder. "That's how it starts, you know. First you're learning tennis and then she's your prom date." He winked.

Derrick just shook his head. "It's not like that." But he definitely wished it was. "We're just friends."

They had dinner together at the kitchen bar—the dining room table was apparently decoration only. This was one aspect of their life together that Derrick found odd, but appreciated it. When it was just their mom and Cassandra and himself, they never had dinner together like this, sitting down and talking about their day. It felt like another life entirely, but he liked it. It made Doug's house feel more like home.

Derrick grabbed another slice of pizza from the box. "Hey Doug," he said. "Was your dad really the chief too?"

"He sure was," Doug said, wiping pepperoni grease from his mouth with a paper towel. "For forty years."

"When did he die?" Derrick asked.

Cassandra shot Derrick a look, but he ignored it.

"About five years ago. I was a young officer at the time. Had no business being made Chief, but here we are. Who knows—if none of that ever happened, we wouldn't be here all together now. Sometimes life gives you curveballs but then you discover that it's just meant to be." Doug took another bite from his pizza and smiled. "So, tell us about your new girlfriend."

After receiving a good ribbing from them all for having a "girlfriend," Derrick went to his room to play guitar and settle in for the night. He didn't tell his family about AJ. It was irrational, he knew, but he already wondered and worried about what they'd say if the rumors were true about him.

He didn't want it to bother him, but it did. Back in Clearwater, he was called all kinds of names for being in choir and theatre. Maybe then, he surmised, that's where the rumors about AJ came from. Teenagers had a way of labelling the outsiders as *weird* or *homo*. He couldn't count the times he'd been shoved against a locker and called a faggot for wearing a band's t-shirt.

As he went to bed, he thought about that. He thought about wanting to remake himself in Mount Vernon, to forge ahead and leave his old school in the past. But he also wondered if AJ was just the victim of those same kind of rumors and meanness.

six

♫EVE 6 - INSIDE OUT♫

DERRICK WALKED OUT TO THE CORNER OF SIXTEENTH AND found AJ waiting for him, leaning against the metal pole that held the green street signs.

"Hey man!" AJ said. "Check this out." He swung his backpack around and, unzipping the main compartment, dug around in the internals. After a few moments, he pulled out three cassette tapes. "I made copies of my favorites for you. I thought about just doing a mixtape, but there's something about an entire album, you know? It's meant to be listened as a whole."

Derrick took the tapes and looked them over. The sleeves were written in AJ's scraggly handwriting, but he'd taken care to write the names of the bands and the albums as well as the song names on the back.

"Wow," Derrick said. "This is really cool." He looked over one of the tapes. It was labelled *My Own Prison by Creed*. "I think I've heard of these guys." He'd heard one of their songs played on the radio in recent months.

"This is their first album. Their new one comes out at the end of next month, so I thought you should give this one a listen before it does," AJ said. "And then this one," he pointed at the second in the stack, "is the newest from Collective Soul." It was labelled *Dosage*. The third, AJ explained, was a classic. "It's not really rock, but still pretty awesome. And their guitarist makes some of the craziest sounds I've ever heard." It's late read *U2 - Achtung Baby*.

His mom had introduced him to U2 when he was younger, but Derrick thought of them as an 80's band, not really new or cool. It was music she would listen to while cleaning the house.

"Thank you," Derrick said, putting the copied cassettes in the front panel of his backpack. "I'll give them all a listen tonight." He appreciated the gesture, and he genuinely looked forward to listening to the tapes, but in the back of his mind, he wondered if this was AJ flirting with him. He pushed the thought away. They were friends, and even if AJ was gay, it wasn't that big a deal. They both enjoyed the same music and Derrick liked having a friend who he could talk with about this stuff.

"What did you do last night?" AJ asked.

"I went to the park with my next door neighbor, Haley. She's teaching me how to play tennis so I can join the tennis team," Derrick said as they started walking toward school.

"Haley Swanson?" AJ asked incredulously. "The captain of the tennis team?"

"Yeah, why? Is there something wrong with her?"

"Not at all!" AJ exclaimed. "Dude, you are so lucky. You get to live next door to the hottest girl in school. I'm going to have to come over to your place as often as possible!" AJ held out his hand for a high five, and Derrick slapped his palm with his own.

Derrick asked, "You really think she's that pretty?"

"Dude, absolutely. She's been my crush for forever," he said.

"Why don't you ask her out?" Derrick asked.

"No way, man," AJ said. "I'd get laughed out of the room. She doesn't even take a second glance at me. I don't think I'm her type. She's into jocks, you know?"

"But she's your type, right?" Derrick asked.

"Yeah, of course," AJ said. "I mean, just look at her." Then, he stopped walking. "Wait. What have you heard?" His face went slack and deflated.

Derrick shook his head, "No, man, nothing bad, I just..." he trailed off, but AJ seemingly already knew.

"This school..." AJ said, his head now held low and his countenance soured.

"No, it's not a big deal. And obviously, you're not, you know..." Derrick trailed off.

"Yeah, I know I'm not gay," AJ said defensively. "But no matter what I do or whatever, it's like a tag I can't get rid of. Girls won't even look at me because everyone says it about me. Who told you?"

Derrick gulped. "Haley, last night. At the park. She told me that I shouldn't hang out with you because other people would talk about me like that. But, whatever. I don't give a shit what other people say. I think you're cool. And even if you were gay, I'd still think you're cool."

"Well thanks man. But still, that sucks. I wish she didn't think that about me," AJ said.

"I mean, she said it was just a rumor. I don't think she believes it," Derrick reasoned. "Why do people think you're gay, anyway? That doesn't make sense. It's not like you wear dresses or makeup."

AJ shrugged. "It started a couple of years ago. In middle school. It's stupid."

"Man," Derrick said, seeing the sadness on his new friend's face. "I'm sorry."

"It's not your fault," AJ said. "And, really, it's kind of sweet that Haley was trying to look out for you like that."

"Sweet? I should be able to hang out with whoever I want. That's one thing I hate about high school. You have to be somebody. Fit in some box. You're either a jock or a nerd or a stoner. You can't just be...you," Derrick said.

AJ nodded. "I like that. Just be you. And screw whoever tries to say differently."

"Yeah man," Derrick agreed. They continued to walk on the sidewalks through the neighborhood, and stood at the stop sign in front of the crosswalk that led to the school. "So what started the rumor?"

"The gay rumor?" AJ asked as they crossed.

"Yeah. How did that even start?"

AJ exhaled. "It's really embarrassing, man."

"It's okay. I won't judge. We're cool," Derrick said.

"Okay. But you have to promise not to laugh," AJ said.

"Okay," Derrick said. "No laughing."

"Promise it."

Derrick crossed his heart. "Promise."

"Okay." AJ paused. "Do you remember the band Hanson?"

♪ ♪ ♪

HE HAD PROMISED NOT TO LAUGH, THOUGH AFTER AJ HAD finished the story, Derrick couldn't help it. It was probably the funniest—yet definitely the most embarrassing—story he'd ever heard.

AJ lightly punched him in the arm. "You said you wouldn't laugh!"

Derrick apologized for laughing and as the bell rang, they parted for their first classes.

In Coach Vargas's class, he found Haley and sat next to her.

"Hey!" she said. "How are you feeling today?"

"A little sore to be honest," he said, rubbing the muscles under his left shoulder. "I'm not used to swinging a tennis racquet."

"More practice and you'll get better. Tryouts for the team are this Friday," she said. "Right after school."

"I'll be there," he said.

Coach Vargas walked in and cut their conversation short.

"Alright, ladies and gentlemen," he said. "As I take roll, I want you to come get one of these." He held up a stack of papers. "These are the Y2K guidelines and preparation materials from the school district."

There was a sudden murmur throughout the class.

"Quiet, quiet," the teacher said. "It's nothing to get crazy about. Just protocols."

One of the last students to get called, Derrick went up to pick up his paper. The packet was several pages with information on how the school system would be updating computer systems due to the Y2K "bug." He'd read all of it before, and had heard about it on television. According to the information, all the computers running on a two-digit timestamp would cease to work after December 31 because of the bug.

Haley leaned into him. "Can you believe this?" she whispered.

"It seems pretty stupid to me," Derrick said.

He continued to read over the pages, flipping through them. There was emergency information on school shutdowns and where to go if the power to the city got shut down. Derrick folded the pages and shoved them in his notebook.

He'd just moved to this town, was making friends, and the last thing he wanted to think about was it all coming to an end because of some stupid computer programmers.

♪ ♪ ♪

After Biology class, he went to his English class and he saw AJ already there, hovering over a spiral notebook, writing furiously. Derrick sat next to him. AJ never looked up. Derrick whispered, "So you really thought Taylor Hanson was a girl?"

AJ's head shot up with a wild look in his eye, his hand a fist around the yellow pencil. "I swear to God, if you mention it again, I'm going to stab you in the face with this pencil."

Derrick laughed again. "What are you writing?" he asked.

"I just had a song idea pop in my head and wanted to get the words down before I forgot about them," AJ said.

"I didn't know you wrote songs," Derrick said, trying to peek at the page. AJ held his arm in front of the notebook.

"Yeah, man. Just some stuff I like to work on." He closed the notebook. "Also, I forgot to ask you this morning. I know it's pretty far, but would you walk down to Sherman Music with me after school today? I need to get some new guitar strings."

"Wait, are you serious?" Derrick asked, suddenly excited.

AJ slumped in his chair. "Like I said, it's pretty far, so I don't blame you if you don't want to—"

Derrick cut him off, "No, yeah, that sounds awesome. But, you play guitar too?"

"Yeah, man. Wait, do you?" AJ bolted back up.

"Yeah!"

"Dude!"

As the other students started filling in the classroom, Derrick and AJ excitedly talked about their guitars, how long they'd been playing (two years for AJ, just over a year for Derrick) and everything else they could get out of their mouths. This excited dump of information and new commonality was cut short when one of the guys in class, a large jock named Ty Anderson sat down behind them.

"Did you find yourself a new boyfriend, *Gay-Jay?*" he

asked. "Hey new kid, I'd be careful hanging out with this homo."

AJ's face went red and Derrick was about to speak up when someone else behind them beat him to it.

"You know, for someone who showers naked with other guys every morning, you're awfully homophobic." The girl who said it was dressed in all black, with hair that fell to her shoulders to match.

"Nobody asked you, Rebecca," Ty retorted.

"Why don't you go sit with the rest of your cavemen friends?" she shot back.

"What are you going to do if I don't? Cast a spell on me?"

"Maybe."

The jock and the goth girl held a death stare on each other before Ty eventually gathered his books and took a seat across the room with a group of other jocks. He bumped AJ's desk as he did, causing the notebook that he was writing in fall to the ground. It plopped open and Derrick could see it was full of writings and ramblings.

"What a jackass," AJ said under his breath. He picked up the notebook and sat it back on his desk.

Derrick turned back toward the girl sitting behind them. "Thanks," he said.

"You're welcome, new kid," she replied. She smiled, her face bright and gorgeous despite the lack of color.

"Would you really cast a spell on him?" Derrick asked.

"He's too much of a pussy to find out," Rebecca said.

"Rebecca here is our resident Wiccan," AJ said. "Which means she worships trees or something."

"How many times have I told you that I don't worship trees?" she asked, rolling her eyes.

AJ laughed, the anger in his face subsiding.

Derrick couldn't help but steal another glance at Rebecca, and she smiled at him when he did. She was attractive, but different. Not classically gorgeous like Haley, but unique. Plus, she had wit and authenticity. He liked that.

The tardy bell rang and Mrs. Rogers started her lesson. Derrick leaned over and whispered to AJ. "I'll meet you at the crosswalk after school."

The rest of the day would go incredibly slowly, because all he could think about was finally going to the guitar shop on Main Street.

seven

"WHY DIDN'T YOU TELL ME YOU PLAY GUITAR?" DERRICK asked as he and AJ walked toward Main Street. From the school, it was about a mile and a half walk to Sherman Music and the entire way, they talked about nothing but music.

"Why didn't you tell me?" AJ said. "This is awesome! I finally have someone I can jam with!"

"I don't know. It never came up," Derrick said. "But I'm glad it did!"

The walk to the music shop took them through the residential neighborhoods, past the large houses that got smaller as they approached Main Street. From behind them, a loud whoop of a siren went off, and both Derrick and AJ turned around.

"It's the cops!" AJ said, but Derrick just rolled his eyes.

"It's my mom's fiancé," he said as Doug pulled up next to them in a police cruiser.

"You guys going somewhere?" Doug asked out the

rolled-down passenger window. He slowed the vehicle down to match the boys' walking speed and sidled next to them on the road.

"We're going down to Sherman Music," Derrick said. "AJ needs some new guitar strings."

"Axe slinger too, huh?" Doug said.

"Yes sir," AJ said.

"I have to take this car to the mechanic shop, which is just a few blocks from Sherman's," Doug said. "Why don't you boys hop in? I'll give you a ride there."

AJ's eyes went wide. "In the back of a cop car?"

Derrick was about to tell his soon-to-be stepdad that they would be okay walking, but AJ cut him off with an excited "That's awesome!"

The two boys climbed into the backseat of the cop car. The plastic seat was uncomfortable, hard against their backs, but the air conditioner was a welcome reprieve from the late-summer heat outside.

"Do you have a lot of bad guys back here?" AJ asked.

"No, not too many. I've probably had a few of your class-mates caught out after curfew though," Doug said with a grin.

"Nice! Who?" AJ asked.

"Can't tell you that part." Doug winked in the rearview mirror.

"Can you run a red light?" AJ asked.

"I could if I wanted to." Doug grinned. "Graduate high school and join the academy. We need young officers."

AJ shook his head. "No way, man. There's no way I'm

staying in Mount Vernon for the rest of my life. I'm going to be a rockstar."

Doug let them out at the curb and told Derrick that his mom would be expecting him home by five o'clock. Derrick thanked him for the ride, as did AJ and they went inside the music shop.

It was a musician's dream. Dozens of guitars hung on the wall, separated and organized by acoustic, electric and bass. There were Fender Stratocasters, Telecasters, Gibson Les Pauls and more. Derrick feasted his eyes on it all. He could spend hours in here and still not play every guitar. Near the back of the store, several drum sets were set up, and someone was playing a four beat rhythm.

"This is the coolest guitar shop I've ever been in," Derrick said, amazed. "We had a music store back in Clearwater, but it was kind of run down, and they didn't have the nice guitars. Definitely no Gibsons. This, though. This is like heaven!"

"Come here," AJ said. "I'll show you the one I want."

Derrick followed AJ to the guitar racks and AJ pulled down a candy apple red Fender Telecaster. The instrument had a white pickguard and chrome pickups.

Derrick beamed. "I have that one," he said.

"Shut up," AJ looked at him incredulously. "Seriously?"

"Yup. Doug got it for me when we moved here."

"Wow," AJ said. "I need a Doug in my life!"

"Come over this weekend and we can jam on it," Derrick said.

"Okay!" AJ said. He sat down on a bench next to the rack. Pulling a cable hanging from a Fender amplifier on the ground next to them, he picked at the guitar, the tone warm and clean. He played a couple of riffs and licks before handing it to Derrick. "Let's hear what you can do."

Derrick took the guitar and sat on the bench that AJ vacated. He sat the guitar in his lap and thought for a moment. He adjusted the tone settings on the amplifier and started playing a riff from the song "Tomorrow" by Silverchair.

"Oh, I know that one!" AJ said, excited. "I love that album! Turn it up!"

As Derrick got to the chorus of the song, he hit the distortion on the amplifier. AJ belted out the words to the song, his voice loud and cutting through the guitar's crunch and tone. Derrick was impressed at how well he sounded and how he made his voice sound nearly just like the singer from Silverchair.

"Wow," Derrick said after he stopped playing. "That was really good."

"You think so?" AJ asked.

"Better than Taylor Hanson!"

"I swear to God, dude. I will impale you with the neck of that guitar if you mention that name again."

Derrick laughed and handed the guitar to AJ. "I'm never going to let you live that one down."

AJ hung the guitar back on the wall-mounted rack. "I'm glad you think it's funny. It was so embarrassing. I really thought he was a girl."

AJ walked toward a display rack of guitar strings and pulled a bright pink package from its hanger. "Ernie Ball

Super Slinky," AJ said, holding the package of strings up for Derrick. "These are the best strings on the planet."

"I know. I use the same ones," Derrick said.

"Of course you do. It's like we're the same person."

Though he had friends in Clearwater, Derrick never felt like he had someone who seemed to understand him, who had the same interests and style. And here in Mount Vernon, he found someone like that almost immediately. For the first time in nearly two weeks, he was actually glad that they'd moved here.

AJ checked out at the register and they left the store.

"Let's grab a Slurpee." AJ nodded toward the 7-11 across the street.

They crossed Main Street, dodging a few cars and went into the convenience store, the door chime dinging above them as they did. AJ paid for their drinks and started their way back home.

They walked back to their neighborhood, Slurpees in one hand and guitar strings in the other, and never once did the conversation stop as they talked about their favorite bands, childhood memories and everything else that came to mind.

For the first time in his life, Derrick felt like he had a best friend.

eight

THE SCHOOL WAS DECKED OUT IN MAROON AND WHITE, THE colors of the football team. Lockers were decorated and the cheerleaders made spirit signs that hung on the walls. The first game of the season was that night and the day was full of a pep rally and excitement surrounding the game. Derrick learned that the first football game of the season was always played against their cross-city rival Mount Vernon Prep, which was a private high school on the north side of town.

The night before the game, students from Mount Vernon Prep would make the trip across town and try to deface the field with spray paint, and every year a group of Seniors were tasked to spend the night at the field to ensure that the grounds remained safe. It was an annual tradition that had gone on for nearly forty years.

Derrick and AJ walked to school every day that week, and on that Friday morning, Derrick carried a tennis racquet with him. A Wilson brand, his mom bought it for him the day after his practice with Haley—the practice that he had to constantly remind and correct his mother was not a date.

"Do you think you'll make the team?" AJ asked.

"I don't really know," he said. "I feel like I suck compared to all these other kids that have been playing for years."

"Well, you do suck," AJ shrugged. "But you'll get better with more practice."

Derrick assumed that was true, though he'd practiced nearly every night since Monday. He and Haley had gone to Paramount Park to hit balls across the net for nearly an hour after dinner. Though he enjoyed hanging out with her, and would do so at any invitation, he didn't think she saw him as anything more than a friend.

She had invited him to the pool party on Saturday at her house and the day couldn't go any slower to get to the weekend. AJ would come over that night as well. After the football game, they planned on playing guitar all night.

On the walk to school, a pickup truck, an older Ford in two-tone blue, swerved behind them, its engine revving as it sped by. The tires splashed water that had settled in the curb from a recent lawn watering, soaking Derrick and AJ's pants. Derrick recognized the pickup almost instantly. Though the paint was lighter in the daylight than it had been when he'd seen Haley get out of the passenger's side that first night in Mount Vernon, Derrick remembered it clearly. As Derrick jumped back instinctively, cursing, AJ grabbed a rock from the road and chucked it at the pickup. It hit the rear window of the cab, cracking the glass.

The driver braked to a halt, the truck's tires squealing in the middle of the road in protest.

Ty Anderson hopped out of the single cab and, gawking at the spiderweb crack in his rear window, huffed his chest. "Are you kidding me? I'm going to kick your ass, faggot!" he yelled as his feet began pounding the asphalt toward them.

Derrick backpedaled but AJ stood his ground, the bottom of his pants soaking from the groundwater splashed on them. "Come and do it, then," AJ said. "It would be your third strike."

Ty stopped walking, the words seemingly a brick wall that he couldn't step past. He stood silently as other cars drove by cautiously with Ty's truck idling in the middle of the street. Finally, he said, "I'm going to get you for this one. You better watch your back, Gay Jay."

"I'll be here whenever you're ready to go to juvie," AJ said, holding his arms out wide.

Ty pursed his lips and then turned to Derrick. "Hey new kid," he said, "don't get this fag's gay germs on you."

"Better than douche germs," Derrick said with a false bravado. He silently cursed himself. He couldn't believe that that was the best he could come up with. Later that day, he knew he would have over a dozen witty comebacks and retorts.

Ty walked back to his truck, slammed the door as he got in and drove off, a cloud of black exhaust spilling from the twin pipes under the tailgate.

Derrick's heart was beating a million miles an hour, and he could feel it against the fabric of his t-shirt. "What was that all about?" he asked.

AJ wiped some mud from the bottom of his jeans. "He's just a jackass," he said, pulling his backpack tighter on his shoulders. "He beat me up in a bathroom last year and shoved me in a locker another time. The school has a three-strike bullying rule. If he does anything like it again, he gets expelled."

"You should let him do it, then," Derrick said. "Just get one good hit in." He mimed a boxer throwing a punch.

"How about you take the hit?" AJ asked.

Derrick thought about it for a moment and then declined. "No way. That dude is huge."

"Right?" AJ said. "I don't want to get hit either."

"Why does he pick on you so much though?"

AJ shrugged. "The Hanson thing," he said. He sighed, his head hanging low.

"Dude, I'm so sorry I laughed. I promised not to." Derrick felt guilty now seeing the pain on his friend's face.

"It's okay," AJ said. Then he cracked a smile. "It is actually kind of funny."

"Did you really have all those magazines?" Derrick asked.

"Oh yeah. Tiger Beat, all of it. Even the posters that came in them," he shook his head, laughing at himself. "I immediately went home and ripped them off my walls. It was so stupid."

The fear from nearly getting beat up in the middle of the road gave way to a lighthearted humor, imagining AJ tearing the Hanson posters from his walls in embarrassment.

"I mean, with the long hair and everything," Derrick surmised, "I can see how you'd think he was a girl."

"Nobody would even have known if I'd just kept my mouth shut, but no," AJ said. "I just had to let everyone know that I thought the singer from Hanson was cute."

They were both laughing now and as they crossed the Paradise Street crosswalk onto campus, they heard the first bell ring. Holding on to their backpacks, they ran across the courtyard to join the rest of the students making their way into the school to start the day.

♪ ♪ ♪

THE SCHOOL DAY WENT BY SLOWLY, BUT AT THE END OF HIS LAST period, Derrick walked across campus to the tennis courts on the southwest corner of the grounds. He'd stopped in the locker room in the gym to change into a pair of Nike shorts and a Lions t-shirt that he had stuffed in his backpack. There were several students on the courts already, doing warmup stretches and getting ready for practice. Coach Vargas stood off to the side of a court, watching two players volley a ball over the net back and forth. Their agility and speed was impressive and Derrick caught himself gawking at them. Finally, one of the players missed the volley and the ball fell into the netting. The girl that missed it threw her hands up in exasperation.

"No!" she yelled, though everyone else around clapped and cheered.

As the two players left the court, Derrick walked up to Coach Vargas. "I'm here for the tryouts, Coach," he said.

The coach clapped him on the back. "Fantastic! I was hoping you'd be out here. Haley already told me how much you've been practicing. Go join the rest in warmups and I'll grab you in a bit," he said.

Derrick did as he was told, and joined a circle of students on the court. They sat on the ground, stretching out and touching their toes, alternating hands, twisting their torsos. Derrick found a place close to Haley and she smiled at him. "Hey!" she said. "Are you ready?"

"I hope so," he said, feeling the tightness in his hamstrings as he reached out with the tips of his fingers. "As ready as I'm going to be, at least."

After stretches and warmups, Derrick was already fatigued and he knew he'd be sore the next day, but Coach Vargas took him to a far court and, carrying a bucket of bright green tennis balls, took one end of the court. Derrick took the other as Coach Vargas yelled out, "Alright, we're just gonna hit the ball back and forth for a bit. I want to see your form and how quickly your eye adjusts to where the ball lands."

Derrick nodded and the first ball came at him like a bullet. He ducked under it, not even attempting to swing, in fear that the thing would take his head off. "Sorry!" he called out to the coach.

"It's okay. First try jitters." The coach threw another ball in the air and launched it at Derrick. Swinging the racquet in a backhand stroke, Derrick heard the ball clang against the fence behind him before he'd even realized that he'd missed it.

He was starting to feel embarrassed, that perhaps he was

in over his head. He was also frustrated with how fast Coach Vargas's serves were compared to Haley's. Perhaps she'd gone easy on him, he thought. Maybe out of pity? It filled him with even more frustration, that they'd practiced all week for nothing. He couldn't even hit a ball at even a medium velocity.

Possibly recognizing the frustration on his student's face, Coach Vargas called him over to the netting. "Part of this game is to anticipate where the ball is going to go and preparing your swing in that place. Don't react when you see the ball coming toward you. Know where you need to be before the ball is there."

"How do I do that?" Derrick asked. It sounded like sorcery.

"Time and practice," the Coach said. Let's try again.

They went back to their respective positions and Coach Vargas served another ball. This time, Derrick watched the angle of the coach's racquet and moved to hit the ball as it arced toward him. With a forehand swing, he connected with the ball and watched as it soared high in the air, over the fencing and the trees that surrounded the tennis court complex.

"Whoa!" Derrick exclaimed. "Sorry!"

"That's okay, that's progress," the Coach said. "Lower your racquet angle and try it again."

On the third serve, Derrick moved into position to his left and gave a backhand swing that launched the ball like a missile to the other side of the court. It bounced once and Coach Vargas volleyed it back. Landing in nearly the same spot where his serve had come, Derrick swung again. They went back and forth like this a few more times before Derrick missed a ball and it clanged against the fence behind him.

"That was good!" Coach Vargas said. He motioned for Derrick to meet him at the netting. "You've got a strong swing, especially that backhand, and when you have it controlled, it's got a lot of potential. Practice is every day after school, from three-thirty to five, so be here Monday ready to go. I think you'll be great on the team," he said and shook Derrick's hand.

Derrick took it in for a moment. He'd never had much motivation to be involved in extracurricular activities, but maybe Mount Vernon would be a clean break from who he was in Clearwater. He felt like a blank canvas, with all the possibilities within reach. He told the coach thank you and went to leave.

He passed Haley on one of the courts. "Hey!" she said. "I saw you from over here, you did really good," she said as she waited for a serve from her practice opponent, the tall black girl they sat with at lunch.

"Thanks. I made the team," he said. Haley squealed.

"That's awesome!" She turned and shouted toward the girl on the other end of the practice court. "Did you hear that, Makenna? Derrick made the team!"

Across the court, Makenna yelled out a congratulations and then served to Haley. Derrick watched them for a few minutes play back and forth. Haley finally was able to volley a hit close over the net that Makenna couldn't quite reach in time.

At the side of the court, Haley grabbed her water bottle

and took a drink. With water dripping down her chin, she asked Derrick, "Are you coming to the football game tonight?"

"If you're there, I'm there," he said, and she smiled.

"Good," she said. "I'll see you tonight then." She wiped her chin with the sleeve of her Mount Vernon Tennis t-shirt and went back, bouncing on the balls of her feet, to the service line of the court.

He told her goodbye and walked home, smiling the entire time.

nine

♫ LIVE - I ALONE ♫

THE FOOTBALL STADIUM'S LIGHTS GLOWED HIGH ABOVE THE football field. Dug from a mound and into the ground, the stadium was a hole in the dirt with an Astroturf field below. The metal and concrete benches were built onto the sides of the dugout hill and it caused the cheers to reverberate through the entire ten thousand seat stadium. Most of the town shut down on the Friday nights that the Mount Vernon Lions were playing at home. They could hear the raucousness as Derrick's mother Dee drove both him and AJ to the game. They sat in the backseat of the Corolla while Cassandra sat up front.

Once at the front gates of the stadium, Cassandra got out and bolted. On the way to the stadium, she had made it known that she didn't want to be seen with him or his "nerd friend."

"I'll pick you up right over here after the game ends," Dee said. She drove off, leaving the boys in the parking lot. She and Doug would have a date night. He had a rare evening off, and they had decided on a nice dinner out instead of joining the kids at the game.

"So now that you're on the tennis team, you won't be able to walk home after school with me anymore," AJ said.

Derrick had thought about it, but pushed it aside out of guilt. After their run-in with Ty in the middle of the street, he didn't want to think about AJ walking by himself, even though his friend assured him that the bully wouldn't do anything more than threaten him.

"Yeah, but we'll still have the morning walk and the weekends. Plus, once the season starts, there's no Friday practice. We can hang out and jam on Fridays," Derrick capitulated.

"Where do you want to sit?" Derrick asked.

"Sit?"

"Yeah. To watch the game," Derrick said.

"Dude, unless you were part of the football team, the marching band or the dance team, you don't watch the game," AJ explained.

"Then why are we here?" Derrick asked.

"To be seen. To hang out. Meet chicks," AJ grinned and raised his eyebrows a few times in quick succession.

Inside the confines of the high fence that surrounded the stadium, Derrick saw what he meant. Students clustered in groups, some just a handful, others nearing a dozen, all in their own bubbles, all in their own respective conversations, like a private party amidst a sea of private parties.

AJ led the way and they climbed the hill, the walkway rising up to the top level of the stadium. The concession stands and bathrooms sat on top behind the stands. From up above, Derrick could see the field, the two teams lining up and then playing. Mount Vernon's defense, in maroon and white, rushed the quarterback after he'd called for the snap and was immediately creamed by three large linemen. The crowd went wild after the sack.

The stands, full of maroon and white shirts, clapped along as the cheerleaders on the edge of the field led a chant. "Maroon, white, go fight fight!" echoed through the entire stadium. On the other side, the visitor's section was cold and quiet, a scattering of navy blue shirts in the concrete stands. The scoreboard on the west end of the field read the score, with Mount Vernon winning by two touchdowns within the first seven minutes of play.

"Bro, the concession stand," AJ said, elbowing Derrick.

Derrick looked over and could see, a dozen yards ahead of them and tucked next to the concession stand, a group of students. Haley stood off to one side, surrounded by some of the girls on the tennis team. Her hair was tied in a maroon bow and she was smiling, laughing at something someone said.

AJ pulled him as they started walking and Haley turned as they approached. Her eyes lit up when she saw Derrick, which made him both smile and flush.

"Hey!" she cried out with her arms out wide. She enveloped him in a giant hug. "You guys, this guy," she said with her arm around Derrick, "is my prodigy! He made the tennis team today!"

The other students, some Derrick recognized, others he didn't, all congratulated him. AJ stood beside him and

Derrick felt awkward having all the attention on himself, but he liked having Haley's arms around his shoulders.

"What are you guys up to?" she asked.

AJ spoke up, "Just wanted to come hang out with everyone tonight. First game of the season, it's always a blast."

"AJ and I have been hanging out quite a bit lately. You should hear this guy play guitar," Derrick said.

"No way, dude. I'm nothing compared to this guy," AJ said. "Derrick is probably the best guitar player in this school. He would smoke everyone else. He knows Silverchair, Pearl Jam, Nirvana, all kinds of stuff."

Derrick felt his face getting even more red.

"Wow!" Haley said, impressed. "I know you said you played, but I didn't know you were that talented," she said. Then her eyes lit up. "You guys should play for the talent show!"

Derrick looked at AJ, who met his nervous wide-eyed gaze with a determined grin. "Talent show?" Derrick stuttered.

"Yeah!" Her eyes were wide with imagination now. "You guys would be great. You could play guitars. It's in December, right before Christmas break."

"I don't know," Derrick started.

"We'll do it," AJ said in tandem.

"Awesome. There'll be more information in October," Haley said.

Some of her friends began tugging her toward the stands and the steps that led to the field. "Okay, gotta go. We made spirit signs," she said.

Derrick realized she had a poster board tucked beneath her arm, and he could make out just a few things on it—#17 in maroon glitter and the beginning of the name Ty Anderson.

"Yeah," he said. "We're just gonna hang out up here."

"Cool. See you at the pool party tomorrow?" She looked at AJ. "You can come too, if you want."

"Yeah, we'll be there," Derrick said.

AJ nodded as well. "Can't wait," he said.

After Haley and her group of friends left, Derrick and AJ watched as the gaggle of girls bounded down the steps toward the field to show off their spirit signs.

"Dude, this is gonna be huge!" AJ said. "Can you imagine? Us up on stage in front of the whole school, rocking out? We'll be like rockstars."

Derrick's hands went clammy with the thought. "I don't know, man."

AJ continued, not paying attention to Derrick's apprehension. "Oh man. I've got it. Let's form a band. Let's get up there and do this for real. I mean, just think. You and me, rocking out for everyone to see. Every girl in school will want to date us."

Derrick thought about that for a moment. As he watched Haley cheer for Ty down near the field, he thought about what it would be like to have her cheering for him. Looking down from the stage and her eyes on him as he played some loud guitar riff. The whole crowd cheering, but seeing no one but her.

"Yeah dude," Derrick said. "Let's do it."

♪ ♪ ♪

THE LIONS BEAT THE PREP TIGERS BY TWO TOUCHDOWNS, and after the game Dee drove them back home. They'd protested, wanting to walk, but she insisted on driving them since it was so late. After fighting through the parking lot, zippering in line to leave the campus, they got home and Derrick and AJ immediately went to his bedroom to collect guitars and amplifiers and went to the garage.

"We need a drummer," Derrick said.

"I know a kid. His name is Dustin Duncan. He's a grade above us. He plays in the drumline for the marching band. Let's ask him on Monday if he'd be interested in jamming with us," AJ said.

"Is he cool?"

"He's kind of a loner, actually. His parents run the auto parts store over on Western Street, and I see him there all the time. I guess they make him work it after school and on weekends, so he's never hanging out with anyone. But yeah, he's cool."

"Okay," Derrick said. He strapped his Telecaster over his shoulders and let it hang. "How many songs do we need for the talent show?"

"I would say at least three. Three good ones," AJ said. He was crouched in front of the Yamaha amplifier, a squat black box with a single twelve-inch speaker as he worked the knobs on the front panel. Strumming a chord on his Epiphone electric guitar, the amp roared to life in a succession of power chords that were distorted to a Pearl Jam-like crunch.

Derrick matched him with volume and rocked the pickup selector on his Telecaster to the bridge pickup, which had more treble and more "bite" than the neck pickup. He played a solo over AJ's chord progression, and AJ stared at him.

"Dude, you're, like, really good," he said.

Derrick just shrugged. "I just practice a lot."

"I'm serious. Do that again," AJ said as he started playing the chord progression again.

Derrick's fingers hammered on the fretboard of his instrument, listening to AJ's I-IV-V chords and finding notes to play over them.

"Okay, we need a drummer immediately. This sounds great," AJ said.

"Let's see if that Dustin guy would be interested in jamming with us," Derrick said. He looked at the clock hanging on the wall above Doug's toolbox. It read nearly one in the morning.

AJ took his guitar off and flipped the power switch on the amp. "Not a bad first jam session."

A few minutes later they were in Derrick's bedroom, lounging on the floor. AJ had brought a sleeping bag, and Derrick threw a blanket down on the ground as well. They talked about music and what songs they'd like to play for the school talent show.

"So," AJ said, his fingers interlaced behind his head, his elbows splayed out, "how long have your mom and Chief Davis been dating?"

"Like two years," Derrick answered. He stared up at the ceiling, watching the fan's blades lazily turn in the low light from the street lamps outside.

"What does your dad do?" AJ asked. "Is he still back in Clearwater?"

"I don't know," Derrick said. "I haven't seen him since I was really little. I don't know where he is."

AJ went quiet.

Derrick continued, "It's okay. They split when I was so young. I don't really remember much about him."

"So you haven't seen him since?"

"No," Derrick said. Then, he changed the subject. "What got you into playing guitar?"

AJ let out a low laugh. "I needed a way for girls to like me."

Derrick agreed. "Same, actually. I've always felt invisible, like I didn't have anything to stand out. I heard Fuel on the radio one day, and I just felt this sudden need to learn how to do that."

"I know what you mean. My older brother is five years older than me. My little brother is eight years younger. I feel like I'm just in the middle. I want to do something to break out of just being the *middle child*."

"I keep thinking about all the bands that came out of Seattle," Derrick said. "I think that's where I'd like to go after we graduate."

"I know what you mean," AJ said. "I often wonder where I'm going to go. If I want to go to college, or if I want to pursue music. It's scary to think about."

"I don't think college is for me," Derrick said. "Though

my mom will probably have a fit if I tell her that. She's convinced that me and Cassandra are going to be the first college graduates in our family."

"You got to do what makes you happy," AJ said. He turned and sat up on his elbow. "Screw it. Let's go to Seattle. After we graduate, we can make it up there, find the music scene."

"You would want to do that?"

"We met for a reason," AJ said. "Maybe we're meant to make it big time, but we aren't going to do it in Mount Vernon. I'm telling you, we are going to be rockstars."

At nearly four in the morning, they'd finally fallen asleep, and as Derrick drifted off, he had visions of being on stage, smoke and lights all around him, and a crowd of people in front of him.

The spotlight wasn't on him, though.

It was on Haley.

ten

♫ LIT - MY OWN WORST ENEMY ♫

THERE WERE AT LEAST TWENTY STUDENTS AT THE POOL PARTY, and Derrick found himself standing by a folding table with a spread of snacks laid out on it. A boombox under the covered patio was playing a mixtape that Derrick had brought and Britney Spears echoed from the speakers, followed by Backstreet Boys. It wasn't Derrick's favorite music, but even he found himself bobbing his head. Plus, he knew that it was Haley's favorite music, so he'd spent an entire afternoon downloading the songs from Napster on Doug's computer and copying them to a tape. He'd labelled it "Pool Party '99". When he'd given it to Haley, along with the track listing, she'd beamed and threw her arms around him.

"It's perfect! It'll be the soundtrack for the whole semester," she had said. "Everyone is going to love this. You're awesome."

Now, Haley and a couple other girls were tossing a volleyball back and forth over the water while her boyfriend Ty Anderson was playing water basketball with some of the other football players.

While Ty was around, Haley's attention was elsewhere instead of on Derrick and he felt a tinge of jealousy inside him. He didn't understand why someone so sweet was with such a jerk. She was bubbly and outgoing and seemed to love everyone around her. To Derrick, Ty just looked like a jerk.

AJ stood next to him, drinking a Surge soda with a bag of 3D Doritos tucked under his arm. He had on a pair of Hawaiian shorts and a backward Mount Vernon Lions hat. "Look at those cavemen," he said, nodding toward the football players. "I'm so glad we're not like that. They've probably got six brain cells total."

Unfortunately, the prettiest girls in school seemed to be attracted to the cavemen, and even Derrick noticed the girls on one side of the pool stealing glances at the muscular, shirtless guys while not even noticing AJ or himself. "Yeah, but the girls seem to like them."

"Dude, just wait til we are on that stage for the talent show. Every girl in school will want to be our girlfriends. We'll have to beat them off with a stick. I mean, you don't even have to be good looking as long as you're a rockstar. Look at Keith Richards. He's been dead for fifteen years and he still gets chicks."

"Keith Richards died?" Derrick asked, confused.

"Yeah, but no one has the heart to tell him," AJ shrugged.

Derrick paused for a moment and then groaned. "That's so stupid."

"But, seriously," AJ said. "Chicks dig musicians."

"You sound so confident."

"What can I say? It's the truth. Girls love rockstars," AJ said.

From the wooden gate that led to the driveway from the backyard, another girl, followed closely by a guy, came into the party. She was tall and lanky, all elbows and knees, with braces that sparkled in the afternoon sun and blonde hair that fell to the small of her back. Derrick recognized her from the tennis team, though he'd never talked to her. Some of the girls squealed seeing another friend show up and she immediately dashed from the guy she was with to join them.

"Hey," AJ said, elbowing Derrick. "That's Dustin. The drummer I was telling you about."

Dustin was short and stocky, with close-cropped dark hair and a towel draped over his shoulders. He was carrying a beach bag stuffed to the brim with what could only be his girlfriend's belongings. He looked like a fish out of water, just as uncomfortable as Derrick.

AJ tugged at Derrick and they went over to Dustin, who was setting his things down next to one of the lawn chairs lined between the pool and the patio.

"Hey man," AJ said. "How was the football game last night?"

"It was okay," Dustin said. "The first performance of the season can be hit or miss. But I feel like we did a good job."

AJ explained to Derrick that Dustin was the drum major for the marching band this year.

Dustin continued, "But after the game, me and Lindsey

went to see a midnight showing of that Sixth Sense movie. Have you guys seen it yet?"

Both Derrick and AJ shook their heads.

"I won't ruin it for you, but the ending is nuts." Noticing Derrick, he said, "Hey man, I'm Dustin."

"I'm Derrick."

"Oh yeah. You're the new kid, right?"

"Yeah, moved here right before school started."

"Dude, that sucks," Dustin shrugged. "But welcome to Mount Vernon."

AJ said, "Hey man, you know that talent show coming up at the end of the semester?"

Dustin nodded. "Yeah, Lindsey is on the planning committee or something like that. What about it?"

"Well, Derrick and I want to start a band for it. Play a couple of songs. We need a drummer. Would you be interested?"

Dustin thought about it for a second. AJ continued to slurp down the Surge. "What kind of music?" Dustin asked. "I don't want to do any of that pop punk crap or nu-metal."

"Rock," Derrick said. "We thought maybe doing a song by Collective Soul or Pearl Jam and a song that we come up with ourselves."

"I don't know, man," Dustin said. "I'm pretty busy with the football season, so I like to spend as much time with Lindsey as I can when we're not practicing for that."

"We'd just need a day or two per week to practice," AJ said.

"And we can use my garage for practice space," Derrick said.

"Well, we'd need a bassist," Dustin said.

"I'll play bass," AJ interjected.

Derrick looked at him with confusion. "But you're the second guitarist," he said.

"We don't need a second guitarist. You're good enough that you can handle the guitar stuff. I'll play bass and sing. We'll be like Rush."

"Rush is awesome," Dustin said. He looked over toward the pool where the girls were splashing around and wading in the shallow end. "Let me think about it. I want to do it, but I just don't have a lot of free time right now to say yes."

♪ ♪ ♪

AFTER PIZZAS WERE DELIVERED AND EVERYONE ATE, THE PARTY migrated from the patio and back into the pool for a giant game of Marco Polo. Derrick was thrashing around the water, listening intently for Haley's voice as he kept his eyes closed, hoping to tag someone. The boombox on the patio was playing a Mandy Moore song from the mixtape that he had brought and it made it hard to concentrate as everyone splashed around the pool.

"Marco!" he called out.

And a whisper from right beside him said, "Polo."

He spun, his arms wild, catching nothing but water and air.

"You missed," the voice said again, this time to his right. He faked reaching once and then dove for the source of the voice, feeling his hands on skin.

Derrick opened his eyes, his blonde hair falling over

them, and caught a face full of chlorinated water from Haley splashing him. She was laughing. "I thought I had you fooled," she said.

Dustin came up from beneath the water and looked at the watch on his wrist. "Have you guys seen Lindsey? I have to be home in twenty minutes."

A couple of the girls looked around. "She said she was going to the bathroom," one of them said.

Dustin climbed from the pool and dried himself off with the towel he'd left on the back of one of the lawn chairs on the patio. He went inside while the rest of the party went back to the game of Marco Polo, with Haley as the new Marco. A few moments later, there was a commotion from the patio door as Dustin came back out to the backyard. His face was ghost-white and he grabbed his bag and went for the gate at the fence without saying a word to anyone else. The entire party went completely silent.

Their collective mouths dropped when Lindsey followed him out the door, in tears, begging him to stop, to talk to her.

And behind her, Ty came out, his face somehow both embarrassed and smug.

No one said a word. Everyone understood exactly what had happened. Haley immediately burst into tears herself, climbing out of the pool and running inside the house, shoving Ty out of the way. A couple of girls followed her in, each of them glaring at Ty as they did.

Derrick and AJ stood silently in the pool, the only ones still in it. Then, AJ leaned into Derrick. "Well," he said, shrugging. "Looks like Dustin has some free time now."

eleven

IN THE WEEKS AFTER THE POOL PARTY AND THE SOCIAL aftermath of Ty and Lindsey's very public outing of cheating on their respective girlfriend and boyfriend, Derrick barely had enough time to breathe. Between schoolwork, tennis practice and fitting in time to play music with AJ and Dustin, it was all very frantic. On top of that, his mom and Doug were putting the finishing touches on their wedding plans, with the date just a single week away.

The rehearsal space in the garage was beginning to get cramped with wedding supplies stacked where it would fit. Family and friends from all over would be descending onto Mount Vernon soon, and everyone in the house was rushing about, trying to get everything in order before the big day. Even AJ had been put to work by Dee, as he'd been the one tasked with counting the cases of water and sodas and stacking them.

On the last Saturday before the wedding, Derrick and AJ

were sitting on their amplifiers in the garage waiting for Dustin to show up so they could practice. Dustin was the only one of them with a job, as he was a grade older than them, so they had to schedule their practices around his work schedule.

Derrick was restringing his Telecaster with a pack of strings he'd picked up from Sherman's. They were a new style called Hybrid Slinkys, from the same Ernie Ball brand that he and AJ both liked. He found that they helped make his guitar sound heavier while giving him a lighter high end for doing solos and riffs on the high-pitched strings.

AJ picked at his bass, a Squier Jazz that he'd picked up at Sherman's as well. He'd bought it with money that he was saving for a car. A bass was more important right now, and he had told Derrick he still had six more months to save money for a car. It did make the practices sound more like a band instead of just three guys playing instruments. The bottom end gave some oomph to the rhythm. Derrick could feel it in his chest when AJ would turn up the volume.

"I've got it," AJ said.

"What?"

"Our band name."

"Oh yeah?" Derrick asked.

"Yeah. We should be called Feedback."

Derrick considered it for a moment. "I like it. Unless we suck. Then people will say 'Wow you guys sound like a bunch of feedback.'"

"Maybe you're right," AJ capitulated and he went back to noodling on the bass, playing a sequence of notes that, to Derrick, started to take a shape as a cool riff.

Dustin pulled up to the curb by the street and walked up the driveway. "Sorry I'm late," he said. "My parents had me take care of a shipment that came in at the store."

AJ stood up and ensured his bass amp was powered on. He plucked a few notes on his instrument, the rumble coming from the amp reverberating through the garage. "It's all good. Glad you're here though. Derrick and I were thinking up band names."

"AJ likes Feedback, but I'm partial to The Hype," Derrick said.

Dustin sat at his drum set tucked in the corner of the garage. Every day, more and more wedding supplies surrounded it. He pulled a pair of drumsticks from his pants and hit the toms and crash cymbal to warm up. "I had an idea, but feel free to shoot it down," he said.

"No, give it to us," Derrick said. "We're all ears."

"Well, we're a three-piece, like Rush and Nirvana. So I was thinking of single word names like that. I came up with Stealth."

Derrick and AJ looked at each other and nodded.

"Stealth. I like it," AJ said.

"Me too," Derrick agreed.

"Cool," Dustin said. "Stealth it is." He counted out to four and began a beat.

The sound coming from their instruments was the most amazing thing Derrick had ever heard, the feeling of being a band the most exhilarating experience. The three of them, here in this garage, it was like a dream come true. As they played through "Smells Like Teen Spirit" by Nirvana, he couldn't help but smile the entire time. So many bands had started just like this, in a garage. He wondered how far they'd be able to take it. Were there countless cities and stages and tours in their future?

AJ's voice cut through the sound through an amplifier they had facing them, and Derrick was impressed with his skills of singing while playing the bass guitar. It really helped to solidify the sound as a band.

After they'd played the song through, AJ pulled a sheet of notebook paper from his back pocket. "I wrote some lyrics, and I think I have a pretty good bass line to go with it. The song is called 'Undivided' and it kind of goes like this." He played the riff that he had been practicing, pulling off and hammering on the A string of the bass.

Derrick looked at Dustin and they nodded their approval. As AJ played the riff, Dustin began playing a beat in time with it, locking in to the rhythm of the bass line. Derrick watched, paid attention to the notes and hit a few power chords.

AJ leaned into the microphone and began to sing the melody that he'd come up with for the lyrics. The song had a very Collective Soul feel to it, and Derrick matched his guitar playing to match that kind of style, playing a riff to match the syncopated rhythm of the bass.

AJ held his hands up. "Guys, guys," he said. "That was perfect. Derrick, that riff, I want to start the song with that, and then Dustin and I will come in after a couple of measures."

Dustin nodded his agreement. "Yeah, I think it'll hit heavier if we do that."

As the boys discussed the song, they played through it a

few more times, building up a chorus and a bridge. After they had it down to what they liked, they played the whole thing through. Derrick loved it. Though it was clear to him that AJ was the dreamer between the two of them, hearing the song that they'd written together made him giddy about the possibilities.

What if they won the talent show?

What if they were to keep this going?

What if they played their own concerts?

What if they moved to Seattle and joined the music scene up there?

As the three boys discussed the song and were about to play it again, two shapes appeared in the light of the opening of the garage door. It was Haley and Makenna. "Hey guys," Haley said. "We could hear you from the backyard."

"I didn't know you guys had a band," Makenna said. "That's so cool."

AJ gave Derrick a knowing glance, as if to say, *See? I told you.*

Derrick's eyes, however, were on Haley. She still had a sense of sadness to her. As she looked down at the ground, her tennis shoes shuffling some loose rocks on the pavement, Derrick realized he hadn't been able to talk to her much the last three weeks after the fiasco at the pool party. Tennis practice and tournaments were quick and busy affairs and she was often surrounded by her close friends, usually with a "no boys allowed" attitude. She finally met his gaze and he gave her a tight-lipped smile.

"What songs do you know?" Makenna asked.

AJ stepped up to the microphone, his voice loud with an echo of reverb through the amplifier. "We know some Nirvana, some Collective Soul," he said.

"Ooh! Do you know that new one? 'Heavy'?" she asked.

AJ nodded at Derrick. "Let's rock their faces off," he said.

Derrick started on the main riff, and AJ and Dustin came in after a measure. AJ's voice wasn't as raspy or breathy as the singer's from Collective Soul, but he did a good job of imitating it. After the second chorus, Derrick tore into a guitar solo, showing off with some finger-tapping moves. He didn't have a wah pedal that Collective Soul's lead guitarist used, but he made do with some string bends and switching to the bridge pickup of the Telecaster which helped the higher-pitched notes cut through the bass and drums. His eyes stayed on the fretboard of his instrument, but he occasionally glanced up at Haley. Though she watched with her arms crossed, she was bobbing her head to the beat. Makenna was all eyes on AJ, and he seemingly knew it, throwing a wink her way.

They finished the song and both girls clapped, Makenna more lively than Haley.

"Wow!" Makenna said. "That was really good!"

"Thanks," AJ said. "We're hoping to win the talent show at the end of the semester."

"You guys definitely will," she said.

"How about another song?" he asked. The girls nodded their approval, and he leaned into his two bandmates. "Alright, let's do that one we just came up with."

Derrick and Dustin nodded, and they began playing the song. It filled Derrick with the same sense of pride and wonder, and as he played the main riff, he decided to give it some flair. Coming up on a note, he pre-bent the string in anticipation of it, a little trick called a "ghost bend" he'd learned watching blues guitarists. As he came to the note in the sequence, he'd have the string bent to the sound he'd want it to make and then pull it back down to give it a sliding effect.

Except he bent the string too far and as he plucked it, the string snapped from the instrument and slapped him in the eye. His guitar made an awful sound and he immediately let go of the instrument and reached for his face. The rest of the band stopped when they realized what had happened. AJ took Derrick's face in his hands and examined it.

"Can you open your eye?" AJ asked.

Derrick did, but it was filled with water and it stung.

"Okay, looks like it didn't hit the eyeball itself, just got you right beside it."

Derrick exhaled, but still kept his hand to it, tears welling up.

The girls came up to console him, but Derrick waved them off, now more embarrassed than actually in pain. Makenna groaned with the end of the show, and told the guys goodbye. Haley gave Derrick a slight smile before following her friend back to her house.

"Sorry," Derrick said after the girls left. "I was trying to get too fancy with it." Looking at the clock above the toolbox in the garage, it was nearly time to close it up for the evening anyway. If not, his mom would be out here complaining about their loud music.

"It sounded great. Get fancy more often," AJ said.

"I don't know about you guys," Dustin said, standing up from the drum kit and stretching, "but that song we wrote is rad. That's what I want to play at the talent show." He stepped out from behind the kit.

"I'm glad you like it." AJ coiled up his instrument and microphone cables. "I've been working on that idea for a long time."

Derrick continued to touch his face where the string had slapped him. It still stung and he was certain it would bruise, though he'd be embarrassed to tell anyone that he got a black eye from a broken guitar string.

After they'd packed up their instruments, coiled everything up and tucked the amplifiers against the wall, Dustin and AJ left. They agreed to practice again later in the week, on Wednesday. It was the only free evening that Derrick would have due to preparations for his mom and Doug's wedding the next weekend. Derrick shut the garage door as his bandmates got in Dustin's car.

As he went inside, he was still humming the tune that they'd written. It was catchy, like an earworm. He couldn't believe that they'd written it themselves.

♪ ♪ ♪

AFTER DINNER—HIS MOM'S SPAGHETTI AND MEATBALLS WITH store-bought frozen garlic bread—Dee and Doug sat at the dining room table going over final plans for the wedding, which was scheduled for next weekend. Receipts, lists and cards were strewn all over the table's surface. The stress of the impending day must have been getting to his mom,

Derrick thought, because she was being snippy and short with Doug as they went over the checklist of everything they would need before the day of the wedding.

Instead of finding himself on the losing end of one of his mom's tirades, Derrick opted to do the dishes, placing them in the dishwasher and then getting out of the kitchen as quickly as possible. Recently, one of his favorite things to do was to climb up onto the roof and listen to one of his mixtapes while looking at the stars above. He would climb onto the storage shed that was tucked next to the house in the backyard and then hoist himself onto the roof from there. It was peaceful up there, no one getting short or sarcastic with him.

He was ready for this wedding to be over and done with so that they could get on with just living life. Lately, everything revolved around the upcoming ceremony. He'd already played in two tennis tournaments—one against Cap City and the other against Murfreesboro—but neither his mom nor Doug had been able to come watch him play due to their preoccupation with and preparations for the wedding. It was beginning to be too much. When he was home, his mom seemed stressed and kept nitpicking tiny details about the wedding and their plans.

After the Saturday ceremony, she and Doug would be gone for four days on their honeymoon, not returning from Santa Fe until midweek the next week. Derrick and Cassandra were going to be alone for those four nights. Even though Derrick had no intentions of doing anything wrong, he knew that the idea that he and his sister would be left alone filled his mom with anxiety, despite how many times Doug reminded her that he'd have officers running beat checks in the neighborhood every night.

So, now, he climbed onto the roof with his Walkman clipped to the hip of his bootcut jeans. His Chuck Taylors gripped the shingles and he climbed up to the place on the roof that wasn't as steep as the rest of it. The house's second story was off to the south end, but just above the garage, he could sit on the shingles comfortably and watch the stars above and the occasional shooting star that would wink in the night sky.

Derrick was fumbling with the cassette in his Walkman when he heard a voice. "Hey."

He looked down, and saw Haley standing at the wooden privacy fence that separated their yards.

"Hey," he said.

"What are you doing up there?"

"Just getting away from everyone for a bit," he said.

"Can I come up there with you?" she asked. "I'd like to get away from everyone for a bit too."

"Yeah," he said. "Come to the gate, and then I'll help you up here."

She went around the side of the fence to the gate and a few seconds later, Derrick helped her onto the shed and then onto the house. Haley sat next to him on the still-warm shingles. The night air was cool, and she sat close to him. Derrick felt his heart racing the way it did every time she was around.

Up close, he saw that her face looked swollen from crying. Her cheeks red and flushed, her eyelids puffy and makeup-free.

"What's wrong?" he asked.

"My dad is freaking me out about this Y2K stuff," she said. "When we got those information packets at the beginning of the year, I didn't think it was a big deal. But he's talking about losing our house and stuff. I don't know. Maybe he's overreacting, but it's so scary."

"I don't understand," Derrick said. "Why would you lose your house?"

"Something about his investments, and he said that the market is volatile, whatever that means," Haley said. "Between him and Makenna's parents, it just makes me feel like something bad is going to happen, and there's nothing we can do to stop it."

"What's going on with Makenna's parents?" Derrick asked. When the girls were at his house earlier listening to the guys practice, she seemed happy and excited.

"Her parents are, like, hoarding stuff like canned foods and water. They think that if the computers shut down, there won't be any way to buy stuff at the grocery store and no way to get your money out of the bank," she said.

"Whoa," Derrick looked out at the dark horizon and watched a blinking red light zoom in front of the white blinking dots.

"Has your step dad said anything about it? Is the city preparing for an emergency if all the computers shut down?" she asked.

"Honestly, I have no clue. I don't see him very often. He's always working, and when he's not, he and my mom have been planning their wedding," Derrick said. "I'm just ready for everything to settle down. Everything has been happening so fast." He glanced at her, and she held her head low. "I'll ask him, though, if it'll make you less worried about it."

"You would?"

"Of course," Derrick said.

Her worried, furrowed brow gave way to a smile. She nodded toward Derrick's Walkman. "What are you listening to?"

"Just a mixtape that I made," he said.

"I still have the one you made for the pool party. It was perfect. I listen to it all the time," Haley said.

"You do?" He thought she would try to get rid of every memory of that pool party, since that was the day her boyfriend was caught making out with another of their classmates.

"Yeah. You put the perfect songs on it. I listen to it when I want to remember summer," she said.

When she said it, though, Derrick felt a hint of sadness in her voice. "I would understand if you threw it out, though. That party was..." he trailed off, not knowing where to take his thoughts.

"I would never throw it away," she interjected. "It's the nicest thing anyone has ever done for me. No one has ever made me a mixtape. And, yeah, even though that party ended badly, I still want to remember the nice things. I still want to remember how sweet you are."

Derrick blushed. He looked down, and he wanted to take her hand in his, wanted to tell her how he felt. But he couldn't do it. He worried that she'd pull away, not ready for another relationship. He didn't want to ruin this moment, here on the roof under the backlit canopy of the night sky, holes punched in it to allow tiny twinkling beams of light through.

"Your band sounds really good," she said, changing the subject.

"It's really AJ's band. He's the front man. The main song-writer," Derrick said.

"Well, I think your guitar playing is the best part of it all. You're, like, really good," she said.

He blushed again. "Thanks. I just practice a lot."

"Makenna has a crush on AJ," she said. "She said that she never really looked at him before, but when she saw him at the football game at the beginning of the season with you, she thought he was really cute. And now that he has this band with you, she's just head over heels for him."

"He's going to be stoked about that. He doesn't think girls even look at him."

"Well, she definitely is," Haley said.

"What about you?" Derrick asked, knowing that the question was loaded.

"Me? Have a crush on AJ?"

"Well, anyone really," he said.

Haley looked at him through the grin on her lips. "Well, definitely not AJ. He's not my type. But I don't know. I don't know that I want to get involved with anyone else after what Ty did."

"He's a jackass," Derrick blurted.

She laughed. "He used to be sweet. I don't know what happened. Actually, I do. But..." She trailed off this time. Derrick wanted to ask what it was, but the last thing he wanted was to keep talking about Ty Anderson. He couldn't imagine that meathead being anything that resembled sweet.

Lost in his thoughts, she pulled him back to the moment with a gasp. "Look!" she pointed at the sky and he saw the shooting star just as it cascaded down and burned out.

"Make a wish," Haley said.

Derrick looked right at her, in her emerald eyes ringed by freckles.

And he made his wish.

twelve

🎵 MATCHBOX TWENTY - ARGUE 🎵

DERRICK STOOD AT DOUG'S RIGHT AND WATCHED AS HIS MOM walked down the aisle to Pachelbel's "Canon in D." She looked resplendent, somehow a dozen years younger than what she actually was in the white dress that flowed behind her. Her blonde hair, which she usually kept tied back in a ponytail, was styled in beautiful ringlets around her face.

Cassandra, in a coral dress that fell to her feet, was crying already, trembling as she held her bouquet of lilies and carnations to her chest. And, Derrick couldn't be certain, but he was pretty sure he saw a tear well up in Doug's eye as well. He wore his police chief formal uniform with its ornate medals and decorations. Usually when he left the house, he wore a standard police uniform. This looked more regal, more ceremonial. Derrick's suit was light gray with a tie that matched the color of Cassandra's dress. The fabric of his shirt itched behind his collar.

In the chairs before them were family members he hadn't seen since he was in elementary school, several officers from the police department, and other friends. Some of the guys that Doug had served with in Saudi Arabia during Desert Storm made it. Two of them had spent the last two days at the house, helping prepare everything for the wedding. One, named Evan, had tattoos all down his forearms and a large, bushy beard that covered his face. He was the opposite of Doug, cool and built like a linebacker. He was also a musician and showed Derrick a blues riff on the guitar as well as a technique called "chicken pickin'".

A couple of times in the last two days, Derrick had sat and listened to the army guys reminisce on their days in the Middle East, fighting against Saddam Hussein's forces. He could tell that Evan and Doug had been friends for a long time. He wondered if he and AJ would be friends like that, too.

Toward one of the back rows, AJ sat by himself in a pair of khakis and a white button-up shirt and a tie that he'd swiped from his dad's closet. He gave Derrick a peace sign and Derrick shook his head with a grin.

The weather could not have cooperated more. An outdoor wedding was risky, especially in the transition from summer to autumn, but the sun shone high above them with white puffy clouds passing by occasionally. There was just enough wind to allow some movement in the air, without threatening to blow away any of the decorations at the altar.

Escorted by Derrick's grandfather, who walked with the bow-legged gait of an old farmer who'd spent decades on the back of a tractor, Dee strode onto the makeshift altar, which was a concrete gazebo in Paramount Park. The tennis court where Haley had taught Derrick how to play was on the far side of the park, nearly three blocks away from the gazebo and the wedding party. Before taking her place next to Doug, Dee gave both of her children a long, tight hug.

"Thank you for being such a sweet young man," she whispered to Derrick. He felt his chin tremble, but was able to keep from breaking down completely. Doug turned to him and gave him a wink.

The ceremony was sweet, and the four of them lit a candle together to signify their unity as a family. After the preacher, Pastor Tommy Maddox from Calvary Baptist Church, gave the newly-wedded husband permission to "kiss the bride," to the raucous applause of the people in attendance, the entire wedding party drove to the Mount Vernon Event Center for the reception.

SEVERAL OFFICERS FROM THE DEPARTMENT HAD PITCHED IN and got the county event center reserved for the big party. Derrick lost count of how many times throughout the day that he heard someone say that they couldn't believe the chief had finally tied the knot.

"Don't let him fool you," Evan told Derrick as they rode to the event center on the far edge of town. "Doug used to be a wild ass, back when we served in the army together. Ask him about Djibouti sometime." Derrick and AJ sat in the backseat of Evan's Blazer as they rode to the event center.

"What's Djibouti?" Derrick asked.

"Just ask Doug about it," Evan said smugly.

Once at the event center, Derrick and AJ found a table with the rest of the teenage guests. Mostly the cousins on his mom's side of the family, the girls were infatuated with AJ, and Derrick did all he could to keep them from hovering over his friend the entire time.

Dinner was catered barbecue—brisket and ribs with all the trimmings—followed by the rituals of the first dance, the throwing of the bouquet and the garter toss.

All the single men, including Derrick and AJ, stood huddled together for the tossing of garter. Doug pulled it down through Dee's dress and chucked it behind his back high in the air. As it fell toward them, Derrick moved out of the way, not wanting to catch it, and the thing fell directly in AJ's hand. He lifted it with pride and cheered. Derrick laughed and they ran off with it.

After the wedding fun, the DJ had the dance floor cleared and began playing dance music. Several adults congregated around two kegs in the corner. The party had officially begun. Derrick had lost AJ somewhere on the dance floor, but he wanted to find his mom and Doug before it got too late in the evening. He'd found them talking with some of the other adults. As he approached, Doug took him in a big hug.

"This is the best day of my life," Doug said.

Derrick looked up at him, and he could tell it was genuine. He'd never seen Doug smile so much or so wide in the entire time that he'd known the man.

Derrick felt the emotion welling up in him, and he'd been thinking about this moment and this question for months now. It came out easier than he thought it would. "Hey, Doug. Can I...do you mind if…" he started. Gathering his thoughts, he paused. "Can I call you dad now?"

Dee looked at him with wide eyes that gave way to a flood of new, joyful tears, and Doug rested his hand on Derrick's shoulder, giving it a paternal squeeze.

"Whatever you're comfortable with," Doug said. "As far as I'm concerned, you're my son and there's nothing that could ever change that."

Derrick embraced him and his mom joined them. "I'm so happy for you guys," Derrick said.

"Do me a favor," Dee said. "Go find your sister. I want to talk with both of you before Doug and I leave for the hotel tonight."

Derrick nodded and went to find Cassandra.

Some of his cousins were sitting at one of the tables on the periphery of the dancefloor, not daring to be seen out there with the adults.

"Have you guys seen Cassandra?" he asked.

They all shook their heads no, so Derrick scanned the room, not finding her. Thinking she may have gone to the bathroom, Derrick weaved his way through the crowd and found the short hallway that led to the bathrooms and the event center's kitchen area. He knocked on the door to the women's room, but there was no answer.

Cracking the door, he looked in. "Cass?" he called out. "You in here?"

Deciding that she wasn't in the women's restroom, Derrick checked the men's room, just to be certain, not seeing her there either.

Finally, he checked the kitchen, where all the food, drinks and alcohol were stored. He opened it, and didn't see her. Turning to leave, he heard a giggle and recognized it as his sister's high-pitched voice. It was the kind of giggle she did when she was doing something that she didn't want to get caught doing. Derrick's first thought was that she and one of her friends, or one of their cousins, was sneaking alcohol. There were several bottles of wine and champagne brought for the celebration, and he could just see Cassandra breaking into them.

He opened the door to the kitchen and looked around, not seeing his sister—at least not at first. When he turned, he saw the door to the pantry, which was propped open, and Cassandra was in there, her arms around someone, her face and lips smashed against another person's.

Derrick's stomach dropped.

His sister was making out with AJ.

"DUDE!" DERRICK SAID, EXASPERATED AND DISGUSTED. "That's so gross! She's my sister!" He and AJ had come outside, out the back door of the event center. The cool night air was a welcome reprieve from the heat inside.

Plus, Derrick needed to get some air before he vomited from what he'd seen.

AJ's face was red with embarrassment. "I know, I'm sorry. She took me by the hand. I thought she was taking me to the dance floor. Next thing I knew, she had her arms and lips on me."

"Please tell me nothing like that has ever happened before," Derrick said.

AJ looked at him. "I swear, dude. I didn't even know what was happening."

Derrick was furious. "You know damn well what was happening."

"Bro, please don't be mad," AJ pleaded.

"I am mad!" Derrick said, louder than he'd intended. "She's my sister. There are so many other girls that are into you. Haley told me Makenna has a huge crush on you. You could ask her out. But, no. You have to make out with Cassandra. That's so gross."

"Look, I'm sorry," AJ started.

"I don't care. Whatever. Go do whatever you want. You'll take attention from whoever will give it to you."

"That's not fair, Derrick," AJ said.

He held his head down in shame, and Derrick wanted to let up, to chock it up to getting caught up in a moment. The entire day, the wedding, what he'd just shared with his mom and Doug, it felt ruined.

AJ looked at the watch on his wrist. "I should probably call my mom to come get me anyway," he sighed.

"Yeah," Derrick said. He crossed his arms in front of his chest, not as a sign of indifference—though he liked the attitude it projected—but because the night air had grown cold with a north wind whipping through the town.

They both walked back inside the reception hall, into the kitchen. Cassandra was in there. "Derrick," she pleaded. "Derrick, I'm sorry. We just got caught up in a moment. Please don't be mad."

He didn't answer, but stormed past her, despite her protests. Finally, Derrick turned to her. "Mom and Doug are waiting for you," he said, coldly.

AJ's mom picked him up a few minutes later, and Derrick watched as her taillights disappeared over the hill back toward their neighborhood. Derrick spent the rest of the evening feigning a smile for his family, but he couldn't help but feel a deep disappointment every time he looked at Cassandra. Though he wouldn't admit it to her or to anyone else, he knew he was being ridiculous.

thirteen

♫ CREED – ILLUSION ♫

Sunday morning, Doug and Dee had their bags packed and were throwing everything into the back of Doug's Tacoma. Derrick sat at the kitchen counter, stabbing at a bowl of cereal with the spoon, swirling the Froot Loops around, creating rainbow whirlpools in the milk. He was still exhausted from the night before, and he had a hard time sleeping, tossing and turning, wide awake thinking about Cassandra and AJ. He was upset, but also sad. Sad that his one real friend in Mount Vernon was probably not his friend anymore.

Lost in his thoughts, he only heard the last thing that Doug said, "...and remember, nobody at the house except you and Cassandra. Not even AJ."

"Yes sir," Derrick said, snapping out of his funk.

"Oh, and one other thing." Doug reached into his back pocket and pulled out his wallet. He withdrew forty dollars. "This should get you two a couple of pizzas. I want you to come home after tennis practice. No going anywhere."

"We'll be fine, I promise," Derrick said.

"You're the man of the house for the next four days," Doug said.

Derrick stared into the man's eyes, and Doug extended his hand. Derrick shook it.

"Yes sir," Derrick repeated.

"Alright. Go find your mom and give her a hug before we leave."

Derrick went back in the house, out of the early morning frost and found his mom in the kitchen with Cassandra. Derrick didn't even look at his sister, he was still angry with her.

"If you need anything, I've left the phone number to the resort on the fridge, along with numbers to some of the officers Doug works with. They will be coming by periodically to check on you guys," she said. Then, looking right at Cassandra, she said, "No parties. Nobody over here for any reason."

Cassandra just sighed and rolled her eyes. "Yes, mother," she said sardonically. "You have said that seven times now."

"Well, I mean it."

Doug came in from the garage. "Alright, you ready babe?" he asked Dee.

She gave her kids one more hug each before the newlyweds left for their honeymoon trip to Santa Fe. After they were out the door, in the truck and out of the driveway, Derrick started back for his bedroom.

Cassandra, rubbing her temples, stopped Derrick. "Hey," she said. "Will you please talk to me?"

Derrick turned on his heels in the hallway. "Why? There's nothing to say."

"Look, I get why you're mad. If I found you making out with one of my friends, I'd be pretty upset too. But, don't be mad at your friend. Be mad at me. It's my fault."

"It takes two, you know," Derrick said, standing in the hallway.

"Look, the truth is, Stephanie, Ashley and I snuck a bottle of champagne, and they dared me to kiss him. They thought he was cute, and they didn't think I had the guts to do it," she said. Embarrassment fell over her face.

Derrick continued his abrasive deflection, his arms crossed. He didn't say a word, just stood there, seething.

Cassandra continued, "I was drunk, and I just did it."

"He could have stopped you," Derrick said curtly.

"Well, he didn't. And really. If it were one of my friends. If it was Sarah or Jennifer—or that girl next door—would you have stopped yourself?"

Derrick didn't have an answer for her, because he knew what the answer was. He looked away from her knowing stare.

"That's different, though," he finally said.

"Why?"

"Because I actually like that girl next door. You don't care about other people's feelings or how your actions affect them," Derrick said.

"I think you're overreacting, Derrick. But, nonetheless, if you want to be mad at someone, be mad at me," she said. "Now, I feel like crap. Do you want some actual breakfast or are you just going to play with your cereal all morning?"

Derrick thought for a moment and relented. "You're probably hungover," he said. He went to the refrigerator and pulled out a package of bacon and a carton of eggs.

Cassandra sat at the bar and cradled her head in her hands, massaging her temples.

"How much did you drink?" Derrick asked. He was pulling out a pan from the cabinets below the cooktop surface on the counter and cracked three eggs into a bowl as she groaned.

"I don't even know," she said. "Me and Ashley and Stephanie got a couple of bottles from the stash. While the adults were doing that electric slide thing, we snuck out back and drank them."

"Aunt Carol is going to beat Ashley and Stephanie if she finds out," Derrick said. "And then she's going to come for you next."

"I don't think she knows. At least not yet. So maybe they'll be back in Clearwater before she finds out," Cassandra said.

Derrick chuckled, his anger letting up.

He scrambled the eggs in the hot pan on the stove and chopped up some of the bacon. In a second pan, he placed the bacon bits and let them sizzle and then folded them into the eggs with some shredded cheese from the fridge.

He plated the omelet on a paper plate that he pulled from the cabinet above him and slid it her way. She dug into it greedily, stabbing at it with a fork and shoveling the eggs in her mouth.

"Oh my god," she said. "This is really good." She leaned

back into the chair and closed her eyes. Her hair, wild and curly, shot out in every direction.

Derrick made a plate for himself and, leaning over the counter, picked at it with a fork.

"I feel like I really overreacted," he sighed.

"You did," Cassandra said.

He looked at her and rolled his eyes. "You're supposed to comfort me here. I made you a hangover buster."

"Well, just call your friend up later and apologize," she said. "It's not hard."

"Yeah, I know," he said. But the pang of embarrassment still lingered in his mind.

"I can't believe they left us here alone. Mom would never do that from her own decision," Cassandra said as she finished her omelet.

"I think Doug is pretty trusting, but I also think we're going to have twenty-four-seven surveillance. I bet there's a cop car parked outside right now," Derrick said.

"Well, even if there is, I'm not doing anything today except sleeping," she said, pushing the empty plate away from her. "I still have to write a report for Mrs. Thompson's class but there's no way I can do it right now. If I'm not awake by five, come get me."

She got up from the counter, thanked her brother for breakfast and shuffled her feet down the hall to her bedroom.

Derrick put away the dishes and the trash, and in the silence of the house, went to the living room, powered on the giant rear-projection Pioneer television in the corner and fired up the Nintendo 64. Today would be a day of *Goldeneye* and *Ocarina of Time.*

♪ ♪ ♪

AFTER A FEW HOURS OF VIDEO GAMES, SHOOTING EVIL Russian secret agents on the giant television screen, Derrick grew bored and shut it off. He looked at the clock hanging on the wall in the kitchen. It was just after noon, and he figured AJ must be awake by now.

He called AJ's house from the phone mounted to the wall in the hallway, and AJ's mom answered, but she said that he wasn't there, that he'd gone to the music shop with Dustin.

Derrick remembered the forty dollars that Doug had left him. Of course, it was meant for pizza, but he figured they could order a couple of pizzas to last them for a few days for half the money, which meant he could take some of the money and head to Sherman Music himself.

Knocking on Cassandra's door to let her know that he was leaving, she mumbled something unintelligible. He threw on his headphones and pressed play on his Walkman as he left the house and started walking to Main Street.

He hoped that, maybe, he'd run into AJ at the music store, and he'd be able to apologize for going off on him at the wedding. The more he thought about it, the worse he felt.

He got to the music store and walked in, scanning the

place for his friends and bandmates. There were only a handful of people in here today, and none of them were Dustin or AJ. He was hoping they'd be here and they'd check out guitars together. Instead, he'd walked all the way down here to find himself alone.

Not wanting to leave immediately, Derrick browsed some of the instruments hanging on the walls, daydreaming about owning one of each someday. He felt at home here in Mount Vernon, but somehow foreign now. Here, by himself, he realized how few friends he had in this new town. He didn't know anyone in the store even these people who should he his people, fellow musicians. But, even the few patrons in the store were older. None of them were someone he would or could hang out with.

"Can I help you, son?" an elderly gentleman behind the checkout counter asked. He wore a pair of glasses low on a nose that was as round as his back.

"Um," Derrick started. "Where are the new release cassettes?"

The man pointed a knobby finger toward the back of the store. "Back there, by the music books."

Derrick thanked the man and strode to the back of the store, where a rack of cassette tapes lined an entire wall. He thumbed through them, checking out some of the new ones. In the section labelled "ROCK," he saw a few that he recognized, but nothing that he needed to have immediately. Instead of buying a new tape, he figured he'd just go home and make a new mixtape from some songs off of Napster.

"That's a good one," a man next to him said.

Derrick looked up. The man perusing the tapes beside

him had long hair, greasy locks that fell down to his shoulders and a wiry beard that hung nearly to his chest. He pointed at the tape that Derrick had in his grip. It read Fugazi.

The man nodded toward it. "They're a punk band from up in Washington. Real raw. Real underground punk stuff."

"That's cool," Derrick said. "I didn't know they carried stuff like that here."

"Frankie Sherman is old school, but he listens to us guys when we tell him what we want to find," the man said. He held out his hand for a fist bump and Derrick tapped it with his own. "I'm Ben," he said.

"Derrick."

"You play anything, or do you come to find new music?"

"A bit of both," Derrick said. "I play guitar in a band with some friends from school. We're called Stealth."

"Man, I remember those days," Ben said. He shook his long, greasy hair out of his eyes, combing it back with his fingertips. "I had some buddies back in the eighties and we had a band. We called ourselves The Conspirators."

"Cool!" Derrick said. He hadn't met anyone else outside of AJ and Dustin that were involved in playing music. "Do you still play?"

"I still have some of my guitars," Ben said. "Sold a few when my daughter was born. But, no, we don't have the band anymore. Some of the guys moved off and Terry died in Desert Storm."

"I'm sorry," Derrick said.

"It's all good. I guess we just all grew up." Ben thumbed

through some more of the cassettes in the rack. He pursed his lips. "It was fun though. A lot of fun."

"Do you miss it?" Derrick asked.

"All the time," Ben said. "We were good, but we had a good time too."

"Do you have any advice for someone just starting out?" Derrick asked.

"Yeah. Don't give it up. Keep playing, keep believing in yourself, even if you're the only ones that do," Ben said. "And listen to a lot of different music. Someone might make fun of you for listening to pop music, or tell you that it's for fags, but you can learn so much about melody from New Kids on the Block or the Backstreet Boys."

"Really?"

"Hell yeah, dude. Some people might judge you, might tell you it's not cool to listen to stuff like that, but it doesn't matter. Take in everything you can and use it to form your own songs. If you don't pay attention to how different genres use beats and melodies, you'll just end up a copy of the stuff you normally listen to and it will get stale. Expand your musical tastes, and piss on everyone else."

Derrick thought about AJ listening to Hanson, and wondered if he still did. He wondered if he had to hide it because of what other people thought.

"Also, don't sell your guitars. For any reason. Sell your eyes before you sell your instrument," Ben said with a half-smile.

"I don't think I could ever sell my guitar. It's the only thing I've ever wanted," Derrick said.

"Remember that," Ben said.

Ben had a couple of cassettes in his hand and said, "Alright, kid, take care of yourself. And if you guys ever play some concerts, post the flyers up on the board up front. I'd like to come check you guys out, listen to some live music."

"Okay, I will," Derrick said.

Ben left him at the cassette rack and went to pay for his purchases. Derrick hung around a little longer, ruminating on growing up and growing away from music. It was sad, to have to choose between living life or playing music. Some people didn't have to choose, though. Some people made it. He wanted to be one of those people. Playing on stage in front of thousands of fans, getting to play guitar for a living.

He left the music store a few minutes later, and all he wanted was to get back home and play his guitar.

DERRICK DIDN'T HEAR FROM AJ AT ALL ON SUNDAY. THE only phone call had come from his mom and Doug. They'd made it safely to the resort in Santa Fe and were getting ready to enjoy an evening at the casino. He spent the rest of the night downloading music on Napster, and went to bed way too late. Each song took close to fifteen minutes to download, but he'd found some stuff from the band Fugazi that Ben had told him about, as well as some new music from Incubus. After school and tennis practice, he'd planned on spending the evening making some mixtapes for AJ and Dustin. He wanted to give them a "style" mix of songs and bands that he wanted them to pay attention to for writing their own music.

His morning alarm went off, and he thought he hit the snooze button, but instead he hit the off button on the electronic clock. When he opened his eyes again, the blaring red LCD screen read 7:50, and he had fifteen minutes to get to school. Cursing, he threw on a pair of jeans and a t-shirt, pulling his Chuck Taylors on as he walked out the door. He nearly ran to school, as groggy as he was. Derrick wondered if AJ had waited for him at the corner, eventually leaving to get to school on time himself.

Once at the school, just as the first bell rang, he saw Dustin in the hallway before their first classes.

"Hey man, have you seen AJ this morning?" he asked.

"Nope," Dustin said. "How was your weekend?"

"It was hectic. I'm ready for our next practice though," he said. "I hated going a whole weekend without getting to jam with you guys."

"Yeah. We're good for Saturday thought right?"

"Yup," Derrick said. "I have some new riffs and stuff to try out."

The second bell rang, which signified the beginning of first period, and the students in the hall started making their way to their classes. Derrick said bye to Dustin, but looked around the hallway for AJ before going into Coach Vargas's biology class. He didn't see him.

He did see Haley, however, and as he walked into the classroom she gave him a smile. "Hey," she said.

"Hey."

"You ready for the tennis tournament this weekend?" she asked.

He groaned. He'd forgotten that their last tournament of the semester was that weekend. He was already disenchanted with tennis. He enjoyed the time he got to spend with Haley, but his heart wasn't in playing tennis the way it was with playing music.

"What?" she asked.

"I just haven't practiced much lately," he said. "My mom's wedding was this weekend, and we've been so busy planning that, that I haven't spent much time at the courts."

"You'll be alright," she said. And then, she leaned in closer. "I've been thinking...wanna go on the roof again?"

Derrick's heart did a backflip. He said yes, tonight, before the words even processed in his brain.

She smiled and leaned back into her chair and as Coach Vargas walked into the classroom to begin his lesson. Derrick, however, heard not a single word of it as his mind was already on the roof, underneath the stars.

And with Haley's hand in his.

♪ ♪ ♪

DERRICK WALKED INTO MRS. ROGERS' CLASSROOM, HOPING to see AJ, but he wasn't there either. Maybe he was sick or something, but he felt like Dustin would have known about that. He took his seat and opened up his notebook. They were studying Julius Caesar, one of Shakespeare's tragedies, and their essays were due. He pulled the pages out of his spiral notebook, sure to tear along the perforations, when AJ fell into the desk next to him.

Derrick turned to say hi and gasped.

AJ's face was swollen and bruised, still red and bleeding, from a recent beating. A cut above his eye was bandaged and his bottom lip was blue.

"What the f..." Derrick trailed off.

AJ's eyes were full of tears and he didn't say anything, simply held his head low.

"Dude," Derrick said. "What happened?"

AJ looked up and said one word. "Ty."

"Come with me," Derrick said. He stood up from his desk and motioned for AJ to follow him back into the hallway. Derrick led the way to the bathroom down the hallway from the English classroom. Once in the bathroom, he leaned against the wall near the sinks while AJ stared at himself in the mirror.

"I was walking to school this morning," AJ started. "I waited for you at the corner for a little while, but I figured maybe you'd come early or something. And then Ty drove by. He stopped and got out of his truck and told me that his back window cost a hundred dollars to fix and he was going to take it out of my ass."

Derrick's heart broke as he listened to this story, knowing that he should have been with AJ, but instead had accidentally slept in.

AJ continued, "I tried to run away, but he was on top of me immediately. He threw me to the ground and punched me a couple of times in the face. Then he got back in his truck and drove off. I walked the rest of the way to school and went to Mrs. Harris's office. I told her what happened and she cleaned me up."

"He should be expelled now, right?" Derrick was angry. He could feel the heat rising in his neck and his ears.

AJ shrugged. "Mrs. Harris took me to the principal's office, and I told Mr. Rawlings everything that happened. He said that since it didn't happen on school property, I would have to file a police report first before the school would do anything."

"What?" Derrick was indignant. "He's just walking around now?"

"Yeah." AJ leaned into the door of the stall across from Derrick.

"I am so sorry," Derrick said. "This is my fault."

"No it's not," AJ said.

"I should have been with you this morning. But, I accidentally slept past my alarm. If I was with you, this wouldn't have happened."

AJ told him that it was okay, that if they'd been together, they both would have probably been beat up. "Or worse," AJ said. "He could have run us over or something. I'm okay though. I probably look worse than it actually is, to be honest."

As he talked though, Derrick's attention went elsewhere. Out in the hallway, outside of the classrooms, as kids dispersed for second period, Derrick could hear the voices of Ty and his friends. And he heard Ty laughing.

Derrick walked out into the hallway. AJ followed him and Ty immediately saw them in the doorway of the bathroom.

"Hey Tooley," he snickered. "You and your butt buddy hanging out in the bathroom together?"

Before he even registered the implications, Derrick's feet were moving, pounding against the linoleum tile of the hallway.

He saw nothing else. As he pounced on Ty, fists flying as they connected with the bully's face, his sight went black.

fifteen

♫ BUSH – COMEDOWN ♫

DERRICK SAT IN PRINCIPAL RAWLING'S OFFICE. MR. Rawlings was a short, squat man who wore suspenders that kept his pants over his substantial belly. He sat into the chair at his desk and read over some papers. Derrick sat across from the desk and sunk into the chair, his head in his hands. He knew he was in trouble, the adrenaline having subsided. His hands and knuckles ached and throbbed. Now that he was sitting here in this plastic chair, in the aftermath of that sudden loss of sense, the weight of what he'd done hit heavy in his chest. He wanted to cry.

Mr. Rawlings pulled his glasses from the crook of his nose and rubbed the knot between his eyes with his thumb and forefinger. "I understand you're new to Mount Vernon this year, Mr. Townsend," he said. "And I understand that Mr. Anderson was involved in an altercation with your friend before school this morning. However, this school has a strict no violence policy."

Derrick nodded. "I understand, sir. And I know it was stupid, but hear me out—"

Mr. Rawlings arced his eyebrows and Derrick knew to stop talking. The man clasped his hands on his desk. "I also know that, according to your teachers and your tennis coach, you're a good kid and that this is your first offense. So, I am not suspending you. However, you will have detention after school every day this week. And Coach Vargas has been informed that you will not be participating in the tennis tournament this weekend."

"Yes sir," Derrick said, gulping. "Thank you for not suspending me."

Mr. Rawlings lifted a piece of paper from his desk and held it out to Derrick. "You will need to have this slip signed by your parents and returned to me tomorrow to start your detention. If you do not return it, however, you will be sent to in-school suspension."

"Yes sir." Derrick took the paper and read it over. It was a notification of detention. He nearly blurted out that his parents were out of town and wouldn't be back until Wednesday evening at the earliest. However, he kept his mouth shut. He already had a plan for this to stay out of trouble.

"You may return to class," Mr. Rawlings said dismissively.

Derrick stood from the chair and left the office. A smile crept across his face as he walked the hallways back to class. Despite the throbbing in his hands, he knew that everything was going to be just fine.

♪ ♪ ♪

"You're going to have to tell mom," Cassandra said from the couch in the living room. She had plopped down, her math book sprawled open on the coffee table in front of her, a notebook in her lap.

"I know, but I can wait til they come back on Wednesday," Derrick said as he pulled two bottles of Josta from the fridge. He tossed one to AJ, who leaned against the kitchen counter. Derrick noticed how neither AJ nor his sister looked at each other, both seemingly pretending the other didn't exist. Derrick, however, decided to keep this observation to himself. "No need to piss her off when she's five hundred miles away."

"She's going to lose it either way," Cassandra said.

"Well, I'd rather her lose it after the return instead of having to get bitched out twice. Once on the phone and again when they get back."

Cassandra rolled her eyes, and Derrick held his arms out. "Don't roll your eyes. You know exactly how she is. I'd rather just get it over with in person."

Cassandra just shook her head and went back to watching *TRL*.

Derrick knew she was right though. For the first time in almost two months, he and AJ walked home after school, and AJ came over to hang out and play music. He wanted Dustin to come over to make it a real jam session, but their drummer couldn't make it because he had to work after school. Derrick then reasoned that having a full band practice might bring too much attention to the house, something he didn't want since they were officially not allowed to have friends over. He and Cassandra had an understanding—as long as they didn't do anything to get caught, they'd have a friend or two come hang out while their parents were gone.

The two bandmates decided to work out some new songs together, and have them ready for their drummer by the weekend. Sunday was their normal practice day, but on the walk home, AJ had said that he wanted to keep their stuff "fresh."

Out in the garage, Derrick plugged his guitar into the amplifier and switched it on, a static hum emanating from the speaker. He strummed a few chords on his guitar and messed with the tuners on the headstock of the Telecaster while AJ plucked the strings of his bass. His hands felt tender and his knuckles ached as he played the instrument.

"I still can't believe you hit Ty like that," AJ said.

Derrick shrugged. "I just snapped. I've had it with him. I've been mad at him ever since I met him. And then that stunt he pulled at the pool party at the beginning of the year. Then today, I was mad when I saw your face and what he'd done to you. But then when he started talking trash in the hallway, I lost it. I dealt with that kind of stuff back in Clearwater, and I don't want to put up with it here."

"Well, I feel bad now though," AJ said. "I didn't want you to get in trouble."

"It's not bad. I didn't get suspended or anything. But, I won't be able to participate in the tennis tournament this weekend. Which is a good thing. I would rather practice for the talent show." He stretched his left hand, the one he'd used to punch Ty in the face, and shook it out.

"Are you okay, dude?" AJ asked worriedly.

"Yeah, I'm fine," Derrick said. He went back to playing a riff to a song that they'd written and tried to push the pain in his hand to the back of his mind. "It's just a little sore."

"Does it hurt?" AJ stopped playing and watched Derrick.

"No, not really. A little, but it's okay. Let's play that new one," he said.

He ripped into the riff, the guitar blaring through the amp. It sounded okay without the drums, and AJ's bass helped fill in some of the gaps in the notes. It was also sloppy, his fingers unable to properly fret the notes. Derrick stopped and shook out his hand again.

AJ stopped as well, the blaring instruments dying to a gentle hum again. "You don't look good, dude. I think your hand is messed up."

"It's just bruised," Derrick said. "It'll be fine." He knew he was lying, though. As much as he wanted it to just be bruised, he could tell that something was wrong, that he'd really done some damage to himself in the process of beating up the bully.

"If you say so." AJ shrugged and then turned the volume knob on the bass back up. "Oh, check this out." He messed with the knobs on his amplifier until it produced a fuzzy, overdriven sound. He played a fast riff and Derrick nodded his head in time.

"What do you think?" AJ asked.

"That sounds amazing," Derrick said. "When did you come up with that?"

"Yesterday," AJ said. "I was hanging out with Dustin. He probably wouldn't want me telling you, but he's still pretty upset about his girlfriend and Ty. So we just hung out."

Derrick held his head down. He wished he'd been invited to hang out with them, but he could understand if AJ didn't want to be around him. "I went to look for you, to apologize," he said. "But you weren't home."

"It's okay," AJ said. "I get that you were mad. If it were the other way around—if I had a sister and I caught you making out with her, I'd have been pretty pissed too."

"Well, I overreacted," Derrick said. "Now play that again."

AJ smiled, turned his bass volume up and tore into the riff.

Despite the pain in his hand, Derrick listened as AJ repeated the riff a couple of times and then started noodling around on the guitar, trying to find something that fit the fast and frenzy bass line. He opted to use a run of pinch harmonics to compliment the bass line instead of playing over it.

"Yeah!" AJ yelled. "That sounds awesome!"

Derrick continued playing the notes, pinching the string between his finger and pick as he plucked it to produce a high-pitched squeal from the guitar. Flipping the pickup selector on the Telecaster to the bridge pickup, the notes cut through the fuzz from the bass and he fell into a nice groove. The pain in his hand flared up, but he pushed it aside in his mind. This song, whatever it was that they were creating, was too good to give up.

A pop from his amplifier pulled Derrick out of his

concentration and the speaker began making a sound like loud static from a television.

"What was that?" AJ asked, turning his bass down and staring at the amplifier.

"I think I just blew my amp," Derrick groaned.

"Oh no," AJ said in the same tone.

Squatting in front of the grey mesh speaker box, Derrick fumbled with the controls on the front of the amplifier, but didn't get it to do anything other than hum and buzz. He fell down onto the floor in the garage and held his head in his hands.

"Yup," he said. "It's blown."

"What can we do?" AJ asked.

Derrick shrugged. "Does Sherman's work on amplifiers?"

"I don't know," AJ said. "Probably. They work on guitars."

Inside the house, Derrick went to find the phone. Cassandra was in her room, talking with one of her friends, and she waved him off.

"Cass, please," he said. "It'll just take a minute."

"Ugh," Cassandra said into the phone. "Let me call you right back. My little brother has to make a call." She hung up and tossed it at him. "Hurry it up," she said as he caught the cordless handset.

The phonebook was stuffed in one of the drawers in the kitchen, and after he found it, Derrick looked up the number to the music store while AJ sat at the kitchen counter, chewing on the calluses on his fingertips.

Derrick held the device to his ear as the phone rang.

"Sherman's," a voice said on the other end. It was an elderly voice, spoken through vocal cords long ago fried by Pall Malls and booze.

"Hi, I think I blew the speaker in my amp," Derrick said. "Do you guys work on guitar amplifiers?"

"No we don't." The answer was curt.

"Oh. Okay then," Derrick said. "Do you know anyone in town that does?"

"Eh, there's a guitar player in town that might do it," the voice on the phone said. "Depends on the amp and speaker model."

"Do you have his information?" Derrick asked.

There was a long sigh, one of annoyance. "Yeah, hang on." The handset on the other end of the line was set down and Derrick could hear a rustling. Then, the voice came back. "Alright, kid. The guy's name is Ben Barnes. You ready for the number?"

Derrick said yes, and scribbled the digits in the gutter of the open yellow pages. He thanked the man on the phone and hung up.

"This is great," Derrick said to AJ. "I know this guy."

From the other end of the house, Cassandra called out, "Are you done yet, fartbreath?"

"Just a minute!" Derrick yelled as he dialed the number he'd gotten from Sherman's.

The line rang twice before the voice on the other end said, "Hello?"

"Hi, is this Ben?" Derrick asked.

"Depends on who's asking."

"My name is Derrick. I think I met you at Sherman's yesterday."

"Oh yeah." Ben's voice went from aloof to inviting. "What's going on, man?"

"Hey, I got your number from Sherman's. I called up there because I blew my guitar amp, and they said you might work on them."

"Yeah. Tell me what happened," Ben said.

Derrick explained how the amplifier popped and then made the static noise.

"Yeah, sounds like you damaged the cone," Ben said. "Do you have a car?"

Derrick said no, he didn't.

"Alright. Give me your address, I'll come pick it up after my girlfriend gets home from work," he said.

Derrick told him the address and thanked him and, after they hung up, took the phone back to Cassandra.

AJ looked at the clock and said he had to get home to do his chores before his mom got home.

"I'll see you tomorrow morning," AJ said. "Don't over-sleep again." He gave Derrick a lopsided grin.

Derrick flipped him off. "My right hand is still good if you want some."

AJ grabbed his backpack and left. After he did, Derrick went to the refrigerator and put a bag of frozen peas on the knuckles of his left hand. He hoped it was just bruised and nothing more.

sixteen

As Derrick waited in the garage, a Geo Metro that looked like a red jelly bean on wheels pulled up to the curb in front of the house. Ben walked up the driveway and met Derrick at the open garage door.

"Hey man," Ben said with a handshake and fist bump. "Show me the amplifier."

Derrick pursed his lips, the pain in his hand rearing its head. He led Ben into the garage and he whistled. "Nice setup," he said, appraising Dustin's drum set.

"Those belong to our drummer," Derrick said.

"You guys a trio?" Ben asked.

"Yeah," Derrick said.

"Respect, man. Some of the greatest bands of all time are three-pieces. The Police, Rush, The Bee Gees."

"The Bee Gees?" Derrick asked.

"Yeah, dude. The Bee Gees. Wrote some of the most amazing melodies ever created."

"I need to start listening to more music," Derrick said. He couldn't imagine someone who looked like Ben, with his beard and long hair to listen to The Bee Gees. He looked more like a Metallica guy.

"Like I told you back at Sherman's, the best thing you can do is listen to as much music as possible. Do you sing?"

"No, our bassist is the singer."

"Nice, dude! Like Rush. I like it."

"Thanks," Derrick said. He pointed at the Fender amplifier on the ground. "There it is," he said.

Ben knelt in front of the amplifier and examined it. "Fender Champion. Great little amplifier."

"Thanks," Derrick said. "My stepdad bought it for me."

"Awesome. My stepdad never bought me anything," Ben said. "He always told me I was wasting my time playing guitar. That I needed to get out there and learn a trade or a skill or something." As he spoke, he turned the amplifier over and sniffed the back of it, near the power plug. "He was probably right."

"My stepdad has been pretty supportive," Derrick said.

"That's a blessing, my man. Cherish that. Not everyone has supportive parents."

Ben turned the amplifier in his hands, checking out the switches. He powered it on and played with the control knobs. "It powers on, that's good. Doesn't smell burned up. You probably damaged the speaker though. I can take it back home, crack it open and see if I can fix it."

"I really appreciate that," Derrick said.

Ben powered off the amp, unplugged it and lugged it out

to his car. He placed it reverently in the passenger seat and turned back to Derrick. "Give me your number. I'll call you when I have it fixed."

Derrick told him the number as he scratched it onto a slip of paper that he held against the hood of the car.

"Alright little dude. I'll get it back to you as quick as I can."

"Thank you again," Derrick said. "And thank you for coming to get it."

"No worries, man. I have been in your shoes. Glad I get to help a little brother." He waved as he got into his Geo Metro. As he drove off, the engine in the little car buzzed like a weed eater.

Derrick went back inside the house and Cassandra stood at the door. "Who was that?" she asked.

"That's Ben. I met him at the guitar store. I blew my amplifier. He's going to fix it for me," he said.

"I don't know what any of that means, but he's a hottie," she said.

"God, can I have just one friend that you're not going to make out with?" Derrick said, immediately perturbed.

"I already apologized for that," she said with her trademark eyeroll.

"I'm going to go listen to music on the roof," he said.

"I'm going to make tacos," she said, turning toward the kitchen.

"Cool. I'll eat later."

♪ ♪ ♪

THE NIGHTS WERE GETTING COLDER, AND AS DERRICK SAT ON the roof, he could see his breath puff out in front of him, momentary white clouds that dissipated with the next one. In his Walkman, he had the mixtape he'd made the day before from songs he'd spent all evening downloading and transferring to tape. The program on the computer that let him download the songs had opened up an entire catalog of music that he'd been wanting to listen to and create a mixtape with. He'd even found some rare Pearl Jam songs that he'd only heard once or twice before.

He'd also made a tape for Haley. It was full of his favorite songs, the ones that made him think of her. He patiently waited for her on the roof so he could give it to her. Toying with the cassette between his fingers, spinning it on its axis, he imagined her joy at listening to it, knowing that every time he heard Vertical Horizon, or Incubus or Tal Bachman, he thought of her. The way she smiled at him, the way she sat close to him on this rooftop, staring up at the stars together and talking about life, god, death and family. On these rooftop nights, it was just them. And he was starting to feel things.

For his entire life, girls existed, but he never noticed them. And then, one day, they were undeniable. Overnight, they went from someone's sister, or someone's cousin, to someone he wanted to be around constantly. An entire population of kids he'd gone to school with his entire childhood were suddenly something much more, yet undefinable.

Haley was on another level, though. She was gorgeous, and smart, and down to earth, and sweet, and all these things that he would daydream about when he thought about the perfect girl.

And she would spend these evenings, just like this one, right here with him. Even if he'd never met AJ, even if they'd never become friends, she'd made him forget all about Clearwater all by herself.

A rustling in the grass below him made Derrick snap out of his daydream, and he leaned over the ledge of the roof. Haley was down there, her face framed between a hoodie and a headband that covered her ears.

"Help me up," she said, and he did.

She sat next to him, and he could immediately tell that her body language was off. Hostile.

"What's wrong?" he asked.

"You're what's wrong. I can't believe you did that today. I thought about not coming up here, but I needed to tell you how I felt," she said.

Derrick's heart fell into his stomach.

"I was just taking up for my friend," he said. "Did you see what Ty did to him? AJ's got a black eye."

"I know," she said. "I'm not excusing what Ty did, but you attacking him like that was stupid. He's not a bad guy, he just has some issues at home."

Derrick nearly did a double-take. Was she really standing up for the guy who made out with another girl at her own party? And then beat up AJ? Were they even talking about the same Ty Anderson?

"How can you even say that?" he asked. "I mean, have you seen AJ?"

"I'm not excusing him, Derrick. But, Ty is dealing with a

lot of stuff, too." She paused for a moment. "His mom and dad separated at the beginning of the summer. His dad came out to her, and now his dad lives in Dallas with his new boyfriend."

"Whoa." Derrick stared out at the sky in front of them, the stars showing themselves the more he stared out. "But, still," he said. "That doesn't give him a free pass to be a dick."

"You're right. And it doesn't give you a free pass to be one either," she said haughtily. "And Coach Vargas told me you've been suspended from the team."

"Is that so bad? I'm not any good anyway," he said.

"Yes you are! And that doesn't even matter. Your spot was pretty much locked in for next semester, and now all our hard work is just thrown away. Once you get on Coach Vargas's bad side, good luck getting back into the good."

Derrick shrugged. "I never wanted to play tennis in the first place," he said. "I just wanted to try something new."

"And how is that working out for you?" Haley said. She was nearly yelling at him at this point, and she worked to keep her voice down. "I like being your friend. I like getting to hang out with you on trips and after school. But, I don't want to if you're going to do stupid stuff."

She'd said friend. All his daydreaming of her, of wanting to be more, he suddenly realized that all he would be is the boy next door.

"Ty cheated on you! At your own party!" Derrick was indignant, both at Ty and the prospect of being just Haley's friend. "Why are you so upset because someone finally stood up to him?"

Haley started crying. "Because I never thought you would stoop down to his level. I thought you were better than him. But, no. You're just like every other boy out there, thinking that the only way to solve problems is to beat them out of someone else. Well that's not the kind of friends I want."

"Haley…" Derrick started, but she cut him off.

"Coming up here tonight was a mistake," she said.

"No, it's not. It's okay. You can be mad at me. I get it." He reached into his pocket and pulled out the tape he'd made her. "I made this for you last night." He was hoping it would be an adequate peace offering, something that would replace the anger that she had for him. "It's a mixtape of songs that make me think of you."

She took it from him and looked at the label that he'd written in his ineloquent cursive. "This is really sweet, Derrick, but it doesn't change what you did. I just thought you were better than that."

He was flabbergasted. "I am better than him! I would never cheat on you, or bully other people. I would be a better—" He wanted to say *I would be a better boyfriend to you,* but he stopped himself.

"I didn't say better than him. Just, better than making those kinds of choices. You attacked him," she countered. "That's what I can't get over. It's that you decided to be just like him."

"Whatever," Derrick said, no longer interested in arguing his case.

"I'm just going to go back inside," Haley said. She stood

up and made her way down to the shed where she'd jump down onto the grass below. "Thanks for the tape."

"Yeah."

She left him up there alone, and he sat for a little longer, pulling his headphones on and turning up the volume on his Walkman, drowning out his frustrations.

seventeen

♫GIN BLOSSOMS – HEY JEALOUSY♫

"I CANNOT BELIEVE YOU," DEE SAID, FUMING. SHE HAD HUNG up the phone with Coach Vargas, which, during the entire conversation, which was more *mmmhmmm's* and *I understand's* from her end, and had given Derrick a death stare that became more intense and fierier as the conversation continued.

Derrick sat at the kitchen bar, his head held low and ashamed. In hindsight, now, he knew that he wouldn't be able to hide the altercation with Ty from his mom and Doug, despite his best efforts. He really thought he'd gotten away with it, and he'd spent the last few days after school in detention instead of at tennis practice.

But then, Coach Vargas had blown his cover, calling to offer his condolences that Doug and Dee wouldn't be able to come to the last tournament of the season, and to offer Derrick a spot on the team next semester.

"You can say goodbye to whatever...*noise project* you and

your friends have been doing in the garage. You're grounded," she said.

"For how long?" Derrick asked. He knew this was a possibility, so he wasn't angry. Instead, he accepted the punishment.

"Until next weekend. No friends, no phone, and no music in the garage," she said.

"Mom, that's not fair! We have to practice for the talent show!" he argued.

"I don't care. Maybe you can spend this week thinking about your actions. You can play with your friends next weekend."

Doug, who stood in the kitchen, a beer from the fridge in hand, simply shrugged at Derrick. "The boss has spoken," he said.

"I'm sorry, mom," Derrick said. "I just couldn't stand it anymore. He beat up AJ really bad, and I just lost it."

"That's not what I'm mad about," she said. "I'm mad that you tried to hide it from us. Had you just told us what happened or what was going on, we'd be much more understanding. Don't hide things from us."

"I was just worried that I'd get in trouble for nearly getting suspended." He cradled his chin in his hands, his elbows on the counter.

"I'm more mad that you didn't tell us the truth. I don't want you fighting, but I will never fault you for sticking up for your friends. However, this behavior is unacceptable," she said. Then, with a huff, "Now go to your room."

Derrick stood from the barstool and shuffled his feet down the hallway to his bedroom. He threw himself onto his bed and stared at the ceiling, watching the fan spin lazily, the blades rounding the base but not doing much to circulate air through the room.

Everything had gone to hell, all at once.

His amplifier was blown, though there would be no band practices anyway because he was grounded for the rest of the week. AJ and Dustin would be upset because their practice and rehearsal time was limited with the talent show just a month away. Except, there wouldn't be much practicing anyway because his amplifier was still with Ben.

On top of all that, Haley still wouldn't look at him, much less talk to him. He'd caught her in the hallway in the morning before class and tried to talk to her, but she turned the other way, leaving him slack-jawed in the middle of the lockers. Even after school, he'd seen her going to tennis practice, and she turned the other way when she'd seen him.

From the living room, he could hear *Sabrina the Teenage Witch* on the television. Cassandra was laughing on the phone with one of her friends as they watched the show together. Scrounging around in his backpack, Derrick found his Pearl Jam tape and shoved it into his Walkman. Sliding the headphones over his ears, he turned the volume up. This was not how he wanted his Friday night to go. As he listened to the sounds of Pearl Jam, he looked over at his guitar, the Telecaster almost useless without the amplifier. He thought about picking at it, practicing some of the riffs that he'd written with the band, but they would sound lifeless without the volume and crunch that his now-blown amplifier could provide. On top of that, his hand was still sore from the fight. It was getting better, the bruising on his knuckles slowly receding, but they still throbbed when he made a fist or wrapped his hand around the neck of his Telecaster.

His bedroom door opened, and he pulled the head-phones down around his neck. Cassandra stood in the open doorway. "That Ben guy is on the phone for you," she said. "I told him you were grounded and you couldn't talk to friends, but he said it's about some business stuff? Anyway, can you make it quick? Me and Lindsey are watching Sabrina together."

Derrick stood from his bed and he took the cordless handset from his sister and held it to his ear. "Hello?"

"Hey man, it's Ben. I'm working on your amp," the voice on the phone said.

"Oh, hey man. What did you find out?"

"Well, it's not good news, little dude," Ben said.

Derrick sunk into himself and groaned.

"The speaker cone is damaged and you'll have to get the entire speaker replaced. Sherman can sell you one, and it'll be about fifty dollars."

"Fifty dollars?!" Derrick almost doubled over. The only time he'd ever have that kind of money would be close to his birthday, but that was still almost five months away. He could mow lawns in the summer for money, but summer had long past and the grass in the neighborhoods was dormant. Even then, he'd need to mow five whole lawns to get that much. "I can't afford that." He leaned against the wall, his head falling to his chest.

"I know, it's not a cheap repair," Ben said. "But, it defi-nitely won't work without it."

The talent show was a month away, and they were already going to lose out on two weeks of practices because of him. He sighed. "Alright. I'll figure it out," he said.

"Cool man. Let me give you my number so you can call me back when you get the speaker. Write down the model number too," Ben said.

Derrick scrounged around his backpack for a pencil and a notebook and wrote down the information. He thanked Ben and handed the phone back to Cassandra.

She shut his door and left him again by himself, this time even worse than when she'd come in. He tossed himself onto the bed and jammed his face into the pillow.

It all seemed so overwhelming. The amp, grounding, Haley, all of it.

Pulling the headphones back over his ears, he let Eddie Vedder sing him to sleep.

♪ ♪ ♪

THE REST OF THE WEEKEND WENT SLOWLY AND BORING, though Derrick convinced his mom to let him use the computer on Sunday evening to look up some information on the internet for school. She eventually capitulated, with express instructions to be done before 10:30. She and Doug had gone upstairs to go to bed, leaving Derrick in the glow of the computer screen in the living room. While he did his school work, some research on Julius Caesar and Mark Antony for Mrs. Rogers' English class, he downloaded some songs on Napster. He was searching for some of the punk music that Ben had told him about at the music store, and he found some Fugazi songs as well as a band called The Juliana Theory. It felt like there was this entire underground scene he'd never heard of.

The songs that he downloaded, he planned to copy them to a tape after school the next day. He'd have a few hours before his mom got home from work that he'd be able to use the computer again.

He wished he had a CD player in his room. It would be easy to burn the songs onto a disc and he wouldn't have to wait for every song to play onto the tape. He had a boombox with a CD changer built in on his Christmas wish list, but until then, he'd have to stick with tapes.

Making the mixtapes also kept his mind off his injured hand and playing guitar. Doug had looked at it, the knuckles turning a nauseating green color. Twisting the digits on his left hand, he determined that nothing was broken, but that Derrick would need to rest it. Which meant no guitar playing for at least a week, if not longer.

Everything had gone to hell, all at once.

While on the computer, he was checking the download status when Cassandra walked into the living room.

"Is that Napster?" she asked.

"Yeah, just getting a few songs for a mixtape," he said.

"Oooh," she said. "Can you download some songs for me?"

"Yeah, after I finish up with these. What do you need?" he asked.

"Lindsay wanted a mix CD with some of the new N'Sync and Britney Spears. Do you think you could download some songs if I give you a list?" she asked.

"Sure," he said.

"Great. I'll split the money with you."

Derrick's eyes shot up from the screen. "What money?"

"Apparently we're the only family with a CD burner. She said she'd give me ten dollars if I burned a mix CD for her, but I don't know how to do it," Cassandra said.

Derrick nearly jumped out of the chair. "Oh my god, Cass, you're a genius!" he exclaimed louder than he'd intended.

Cassandra gave him a confused look, but Derrick was already excited. "How many other people do you know that need CD's like this?"

"I don't know, a few maybe. Why?"

"I need to make fifty dollars to get my amp fixed," he explained. "This is going to be so easy. If we get ten people to give us ten bucks each, we both make fifty dollars. We can take orders at school tomorrow and have the discs delivered on Friday."

"Fifty dollars?" she asked. "What if we did that every week? That's fifty dollars before every weekend. I could literally buy a new outfit every Saturday."

He did a quick calculation in his head. At just ten discs per week, he could make two every night and have them all ready for the end of the week. He could have Cassandra take the orders, and then he could spend the evenings downloading the songs. With some luck, most kids who wanted pop music would invariably want some of the same songs, so he'd only have to download them once.

"Yeah, this is the best idea you've ever had," he said. "Tomorrow, I need you to get as many orders as possible. I need to get my amp fixed before I'm ungrounded so I can be ready to practice with my band again."

Cassandra agreed to the plan and Derrick began downloading the songs from the list she'd given him. Luckily, he had a couple of them from the mixtapes he'd already made for Haley. He looked at the clock in the bottom corner of the screen, and it read just before ten. He could get a couple more songs in before he had to shut off the computer.

He had an epiphany, though. No one needed the telephone while they were all asleep, so he could keep the computer connected to the internet all night. He could set all the songs he needed to download and have them ready in the morning. This idea was getting easier and easier every moment.

As he got the songs on Cassandra's list in the download queue in Napster, his ICQ messenger application dinged and he opened the window that he'd minimized at the bottom of the screen. It was from AJ.

AJ: Hey man. Are you doing that assignment about Caesar?

Derrick: Yeah, just finished.

AJ: We jamming tomorrow?

Derrick: I'm grounded. Mom found out about the fight. Plus my hand is still jacked. :(

AJ: Damn dude. I'm sorry. How long till you can play?

Derrick: Not til next weekend

AJ: …

Derrick: I know.

But I'll have my amp fixed before then so I'll be ready to practice for the talent show.

AJ: Cool dude. Meet me at the corner in the morning. I have an idea for the band.

Derrick: Alright. See you in the am.

DERRICK LOGGED OFF CHAT AND, WITH HIS LIST OF SONGS SET to download, turned off the monitor. He would get up to check it in the morning to make sure all the songs downloaded.

In his bedroom, he pulled his clothes off and threw them into the basket in the corner. He crawled under his sheets, but sleep was hard to harness. All he could think about was that he'd just found the solution to all his problems.

Well, all except one.

Because no matter how much money he could make from selling the burned CDs at school, no matter how quickly these two weeks could go by, Haley was still not talking to him. He passed her in the hall and she barely looked at him. When she once smiled and lit up when he walked into Biology class, she barely noticed when he took his seat next to her.

That was the one thing that stung the most. As he fell

asleep, he thought about her, on the roof. In his half-conscious visions, in the dream-state halfway between awake and asleep, he gave her the mixtape. Haley nestled her head on his shoulder and then, as he turned his head to hers, she leaned in and kissed him.

eighteen

♫ PEARL JAM – SPIN THE BLACK CIRCLE ♫

DERRICK MET AJ AT THE CORNER ON THEIR WALK TO SCHOOL. After all weekend of being grounded, of not being able to talk on the phone or see his friends, it was nice to finally feel like he was free from the house and out from the tyranny of groundation.

"Alright, so I have this idea for the band," AJ said excitedly. "You know, we are going to win this talent show." As he talked, he moved his hands like he'd had a dozen cups of coffee before school. "I mean, that's a given. We're just too good. Anyway, once that happens, everybody will want more music from us. They'll want us to play concerts and all kinds of stuff. Well, for Christmas, I'm going to ask for a four-track recorder. What if we spent the entire Christmas break recording a demo tape?"

Derrick thought about it. Though he wasn't as certain that they'd actually win the competition, there was a definite allure to recording their songs. "That sounds awesome," he said. "We have five songs now. That's enough for an EP."

"Exactly. We can record it over the break, and then when we get back to school, we can sell them," AJ said.

"Do you think people would actually buy them?" Derrick asked.

"When we win this talent show, we'll be the most popular guys in school," AJ said.

"What if we don't go back?" Derrick asked.

"What do you mean?"

"What if this Y2K thing really does knock out all the computer systems and they can't open the schools back up?" He kicked an aluminum can in the street and it bounced against the concrete curb.

"I don't think that's actually going to happen. My dad says the media is just trying to scare us all into buying stuff. But even if it does happen, if all the computers go out, I've thought of that already. Tapes are analog. So, the only way to listen to music will be cassettes, and the kids at our school will want music anyway. Either way, it's a win-win!" AJ said.

"Well, I hope you're right," Derrick said.

As they walked to school in the late autumn morning, their breath visible in the cold air as they spoke, Derrick was glad to be out of the house. "I need your help with something," he said.

"What?"

"Ask everyone you know if they want a mix CD. Any songs they want. Ten songs for ten dollars. I'm gonna make these custom mixes for people so I can get my amplifier fixed," Derrick said.

"That's a great idea!" AJ said. "You have a CD burner?"

"Yeah, Doug's computer has one. Apparently he has to burn CDs to back up files for work or something. Last night, I left the computer on all night and was able to download twelve songs. I'm hoping a bunch of kids want the same songs so it'll go faster. But, if I can get ten orders, I'll have enough money to fix my amp."

"Dude, yes. If we get enough orders, you can buy a whole new amp! What if we get to this talent show and you're playing through a Marshall stack?" AJ said.

Derrick thought about it. That would be the ultimate rockstar look, standing in front of a giant tower of speakers. Though, even at ten dollars per custom CD, he would have to sell a CD to nearly every kid in the tenth grade in order to make something like that happen.

"Let's just get enough to fix the amp I've got now, and we can worry about something bigger later," he said.

"Alright. I'll ask some people in my classes if they want a CD. Ten bucks?" AJ asked.

"That's it. Hopefully we can get enough so that I can fix my amp and we can start practicing again. I like the idea of recording our songs too," Derrick said.

They crossed the street to the campus and made it just as the bell rang. Inside the halls, Derrick saw Haley in passing as he left his locker to Coach Vargas's biology class, and she quickly turned away from him. Beyond anything else—his bruised hand, his busted amplifier—their friendship was the one thing he wanted fixed.

♪ ♪ ♪

AJ FOUND DERRICK ON THE WAY TO THE CAFETERIA FOR lunch and handed him a handful of folded sheets of notebook paper.

"What's this?" Derrick asked.

"These are the lists of songs that everybody wants," AJ answered.

Derrick took the papers in his hand and looked them over. There were at least three dozen sheets of notebook paper, each one with a list of songs scribbled on it.

"Oh my god," Derrick said as they walked into the cafeteria. As they stood in line, Derrick read each one. The initial shock of the amount of orders here wore off when he noticed that several of the requests had many of the same songs.

"This is incredible," he finally said. He noticed in the top corner of some of the pages, a check mark had been crudely scrawled. "What are these check marks?"

"I was waiting for you to ask," AJ said, and from his pocket revealed a wad of cash. "Those are the ones that have already paid."

Derrick's eyes went wide. "You got some of them to already pay?"

"Yeah man. I figured you'd need the amp fixed as soon as possible."

"How did you get so many?" Derrick asked.

"I just told everyone that when Y2K hits, the internet will go down and they won't be able to get music off Napster anymore."

Derrick nearly hugged him. "That is almost evil, but so awesome. Wow, man!"

He counted the cash, low in his hands and close to his torso, the collection of fives and tens nearly spilling out of his grip. Of the thirty orders, over a dozen had prepaid, giving him more than enough money to pay for his amplifier repair.

He split off twenty dollars and handed it to AJ. "Here, man," he said.

AJ declined. "No way. You're doing the work, I'm just getting the sales."

"Take it, please. Without you, I wouldn't even have all this. Please," he said. "I only needed fifty dollars to fix the amp."

After a heartbeat, AJ took the money.

"Let's go to Sherman's after school. We can pay for the amp, plus I'm going to need a lot of blank CDs," Derrick said.

"You know, with a few more sales, we can get you a wah pedal too," AJ said. "You'll sound more like Collective Soul when we play at the talent show."

Derrick's eyes went wide. "Oh my god, yes."

He couldn't believe that they'd opened up this revenue stream in order to buy the effects pedals, strings, everything they'd need for their band. Money, aside from the hundred dollars or so that he'd receive for birthday gifts, was almost always out of reach. Thus, the ability to purchase items such as effects pedals and amplifiers—the things that would catapult him from novice guitarist to something that resembled an actual musician—was usually left as the stuff of daydreams. Now, however? It was within his grasp.

And if they were to really record a demo tape over the

break, he would need those kinds of things to make them sound legit, and not just like a copy-cat garage band.

As they talked, they took their food in the line, piling slices of pizza, a bowl of fruit and cartons of chocolate milk onto their lunch trays and sat at the end of one of the long tables that ran in parallel rows in the large, open cafeteria. A girl sat next to Derrick.

"Hey," she said.

Derrick looked up to see Rebecca as she slid into the seat. Her hair, dyed black, with the blonde roots coming through at the part, hung to her shoulders in wavy locks. It clashed against her ivory white skin. Pushing a lock of hair behind her ear, she showed an ear with several piercings.

"Hey Rebecca," Derrick said.

"I heard you guys are selling custom mix CDs," she said. "Can I buy one?"

"Yeah, of course," Derrick said. "Ten songs for ten dollars."

She handed him a slip of notebook paper that had been ripped from a spiral notebook, the bits where it had been torn still hanging. Derrick unfolded it and read the list.

It was full of the bands he and AJ listened to, the first was a song called "Spin the Black Circle" by Pearl Jam.

"This is a great list," Derrick said. "I have all these on a mixtape."

AJ took the paper and read it over as well. "If only more girls liked this music," he pondered, folding it and handing it back to Derrick. "We'd have a lot less crappy music on the radio."

"Yeah, well, I'm glad they don't. I like being different," she said.

Derrick added the sheet to his stack of other orders. "I'll get this to you on Friday."

"Great. And," she said, getting up from the seat, "if you guys think all the girls like the wrong kind of music, maybe you're chasing the wrong kind of girls."

Rebecca started to walk away, but Derrick called out.

"Hey, Rebecca."

She turned around.

"Do you want to come listen to our band practice on Sunday?" he asked. Before she answered, the words continued to spill from his mouth. "We play stuff like you like."

"Sure," she said. "Where?"

Derrick ripped a corner from a sheet of paper and scribbled his address on it. Handing it to her, he said, "We practice around two o'clock. Come hang out. You'll like it."

"Cool. Yeah, I'll come listen," she said.

"Cool," Derrick said.

He sat back down and AJ stared at him, his eyebrows raised. He bit from his pizza and said between chews, "How do you do that?"

"Do what?"

"Talk to girls without them looking at you like you're an alien."

Derrick ate his pizza as well. "What are you talking about? I feel like a bumbling idiot every time a girl talks to me."

"Well, find Rebecca's list again and let's look at the songs," AJ said.

"Why?"

"Because she's gonna fall in love with you if we learn one."

They continued to eat, and after a few minutes the conversation shifted away from girls and to their plans to record their demo over the break. However, Derrick let his eyes wander over to the table where Rebecca sat with a couple of the other "punk" kids, and every time he did, his eyes met hers, just for a moment before they both looked away again.

She wasn't usually his type, but Derrick couldn't help but wonder what it would be like to date a girl like her. She was someone that he could talk about music with, who he didn't have to be somebody else or become something he didn't want to be just to impress her. The more he looked at her, the more he saw how beautiful she really was.

He couldn't wait for Sunday.

nineteen

♫ FILTER – TAKE A PICTURE ♫

DERRICK PLUGGED HIS GUITAR INTO THE AMPLIFIER AND turned the unit on. It hummed to life and he strummed a chord. It sounded like new. No, better than new. The new speaker was clear and punchy and seemed to hold more bottom end than the original stock one did. Even better, his hand felt great, and he gripped the neck of his instrument without any pain for the first time in weeks.

"That sounds really good," AJ said as he dialed in his bass.

"Yeah, I'm glad Ben got it to work." Derrick stepped on the Dunlop wah pedal at his foot and rocked the switch back and forth. His guitar's tone followed the motion, creating an effect that mimicked the sweeping sound from a Collective Soul album. He grinned with joy. It was perfect.

The pedal cost him just over a hundred dollars at Sherman's, but it was well worth the price. He'd made so many mix CDs—with even more orders to be fulfilled—that it took up nearly all his time making them. Fortunately, he only had to download the songs once. The downloading took up the most time, with each song taking as much as twenty minutes to transfer from Napster. But, once he had that done, it was easy to mix the songs in Winamp and burn them to a disc.

Dustin pulled up to the driveway and walked in through the open garage door. "Some of the girls at school said you invited them to come listen to us," he said as he went to his drum kit. He hit the snare to tune it and made sure his cymbals were tightened to their stands.

Derrick's eyes went wide. "I mean, I invited Rebecca," he said. "But that's about it."

"Well, Jessica and Leah said they were coming today too. Looks like we're going to have our first concert," Dustin said. He pounded a beat on his drums and crashed the cymbals. "Which, I don't mind. Leah's so hot."

"This is gonna be awesome," AJ said with a glint in his eyes. He immediately began running his fingers through his hair, making sure it fell in all the right directions. "What songs should we play?"

Derrick ran through their list in his head. He came up with five songs that they could play for the girls when they showed up, a mix of covers with two of the songs that they'd written themselves. His hands were already sweating with the idea of playing in front of an audience. What if he missed a note or embarrassed himself in front of them? What if a string broke again like last time they'd had an audience?

He didn't have much time to dwell on his nervousness, because just as they were tuning their instruments and talking about the setlist they'd practice today, a car pulled up to the curb, its brakes squealing as it did. Three girls got out of the boxy Ford and strolled up the driveway. Rebecca and the two other girls approached the garage.

Rebecca wore a tight black Mercyful Fate t-shirt over a long sleeve shirt. Her thumbs poked through holes in the sleeves. A black choker around her neck completed the outfit, though she didn't wear the black lipstick that she normally had on at school. The two girls that accompanied her were similarly dressed, but, in Derrick's mind, neither of them pulled it off as well as Rebecca.

"I hope you don't mind, but Leah and Jessica wanted to come listen to you guys too, and I told them it would be alright," she said.

"Yeah," Derrick gulped. "Yeah, it's cool."

"So what is your band called?" Leah asked. Though Rebecca wasn't very tall herself, Leah was even shorter, coming up to just Rebecca's chin. She looked absolutely miniscule next to Jessica, who was tall and curvy.

"Stealth," AJ answered into the microphone, his voice reverberating through the speaker that his microphone plugged into.

"Cool," Leah said.

AJ leaned away from the microphone stand and said to Derrick and AJ, "Alright, let's run through 'Heavy' and then that new one that we wrote."

Dustin nodded and counted off for Derrick. After the fourth beat, Derrick tore into the main riff of the Collective Soul song, using the wah pedal at his foot to accentuate the chords. It sounded amazing, just like the record. The girls watching seemed to be impressed as they looked at each other, nodding their heads to the tune.

AJ beefed up the fuzz in his amplifier to distort the bass lines to make it sound heavier and fuller, which allowed Derrick to play a solo over the bridge. They finished up the song and whatever nervousness Derrick felt had completely subsided, though he couldn't help but notice Rebecca watching him during the entire song.

"That was so good!" Leah exclaimed.

"Yeah, that was, like, better than anyone else," Jessica agreed.

AJ bowed dramatically and then said, "We're going to play one that we wrote."

As he spoke a couple more kids, freshmen that Derrick recognized from the hallways, walked up the driveway. "Hey man, we could hear you from across the street," one of them said. His curly red hair sprayed out in every direction from his head. "Thought we'd come listen to you practice."

"Yeah, are you guys playing the talent show?" the other asked.

There was now nearly a half dozen students in the driveway, turning this practice session into an impromptu concert, and Derrick could tell that AJ was loving it.

"Yes we are," AJ said into the microphone. "And now we're going to play a song that my best friend here Derrick wrote."

Derrick began the riff for the new song, with the drums coming in behind him. The kids in the driveway began bobbing their heads and moving to the groove. AJ's bass thumped in his chest and Derrick kept his eyes down on his guitar's fretboard, not in fear of missing a note, but keeping his eyes averted from Rebecca's gaze.

As they finished the song, Dustin pounding on the crash cymbals and AJ making his bass rumble, the audience clapped.

Rebecca called out, "Do you guys know 'Shimmer' by Fuel?"

AJ nodded. "We do. Wanna hear it?"

"Absolutely!" Her eyes lit up. She was normally quiet at school, but here, her face beamed with an excitement that Derrick had never seen before. She was actually quite gorgeous when she wasn't brooding.

AJ nodded to Derrick and he began the guitar intro to the song. He looked up at Rebecca who was absolutely beaming. She smiled at him as he played, and his stomach turned in knots. He thought about Haley next door, and how she hadn't spoken to him since that night on the roof, how he'd been completely enamored with her since he saw her that first night they'd moved to Mount Vernon. But, now, here was Rebecca, who—though much different from Haley— he felt was more his type. Someone he could talk music with; someone that understood the things he was into. As they played the song she had requested, her infatuation with him apparent, Derrick felt it reciprocated in himself.

Just as he started into the guitar solo of the song, Derrick's playing was cut short by the sound of a siren at the road. He looked up from his guitar to see a police car pull up to the driveway, the lights spinning on the roof. The officer got out and began walking up the driveway. It was Doug, in uniform.

He made a motion with his hand and mouthed, "Cut the music." AJ and Dustin stopped as well, leaving only the hum from the amplifiers and the murmurs from the students who congregated in front of the garage.

"Sorry guys," Doug said. "We got a call of a noise disturbance over dispatch. You boys are going to have to cut it early today."

Derrick groaned. They were just getting into a groove. His nervousness had subsided and he was beginning to enjoy

Doug turned to the students in the driveway behind him. "Show's over. Time for you kids to go home." Something in Rebecca's face when he spoke looked like physical pain. Though Derrick could see it, see her eyes averted from the police officer, he didn't understand her reaction.

The six high school students who'd come to watch and listen to their band made their way out from the garage, with Rebecca and her friends climbing in the Ford sedan and driving off. Derrick pulled his guitar off his shoulder and flipped off his amplifier.

"Hey, come here a second," Doug said, motioning for Derrick.

Derrick walked out of the garage and followed Doug to the idling police cruiser.

"I don't mind you guys using the garage as a rehearsal space, but if I get a call, I've got to shut you down," he said.

Derrick said, "I understand. We were probably a bit

louder this time than normal because we had people from school who wanted to come listen."

Doug looked up for a moment and then back to Derrick. His eyes were stern, as was his tone. "I trust you to make good decisions on your own. But, I want you to know right now. Rebecca Winters is not welcome at this house. Ever. Do you understand?"

Derrick was taken aback, but instinctively said, "Yes sir."

"Good. I have to get back to the station," Doug said. "You boys should go ahead and pack it up for the day, though."

Derrick acknowledged and said goodbye as Doug got in his car and drove off. Derrick trudged up the driveway back into the garage where his bandmates waited in confusion.

"Everything alright?" AJ asked. "He looked pissed."

"What was that about?" Dustin said.

"No," Derrick said. "We have to find a new practice space."

♪ ♪ ♪

AFTER A PHONE CALL TO HIS PARENTS THAT NEARLY DEVOLVED into him flat-out begging, Dustin hung up the phone and leaned against the wall. "They said yes," he said with a sigh.

After Doug had told them about the disturbance call, they'd come inside the house and Dustin called his parents to ask them if they could set up a rehearsal space in the warehouse area of their shop. Though reluctant at first, his dad finally capitulated.

Derrick and AJ sighed almost in unison and then they all high-fived each other.

"It's going to take a few trips to get all our equipment over there," Dustin said.

"We'll help tear your drum kit down and pack it up first," AJ said.

"That'll be the hardest part. The speakers are heavy, but they don't take as much time to set up," Derrick said.

The bed of Dustin's Ford Ranger was large enough to fit their equipment in a couple of trips, so they got to work immediately on the drums. Once they were secured in the bed of the pickup, they hopped in, with AJ taking the cramped back seat.

On the drive over, Dustin put in a tape and they discussed the instrumentation and how they'd record their demo over the break. From the backseat, AJ talked animatedly about the process, about how they'd be able to record their tracks independently and be able to overdub multiple guitars.

They were able to get all their equipment moved over to the warehouse behind the auto parts store in two trips and set everything up to get ready for their next practice. The talent show was coming in just a few weeks, and they wanted to get a few more rehearsals in before it happened. Then, Christmas break would be on them and they'd spend every day possible recording their demo tape.

Derrick wondered if this thing—this band, the music, all of it—was something more than just a project for them to perform at a school talent show. That they had something special here, something that could take them out of their small town. Something that could turn them famous, like the bands on VH1 and playing big sold-out shows in front of thousands of people.

In the back of his mind, though, he thought about Ben. Though grateful that he was around and able to help him with the amplifier and get it back to working, Derrick couldn't help but wonder where it had gone wrong for him, why his band didn't go any further than Mount Vernon. Surely they'd had the same aspirations, to play somewhere other than garages and school talent shows.

Or maybe, it doesn't go wrong.

Maybe, Derrick thought, it's more like getting lucky. When someone catches a lightning bolt and rides up into the sky, do the people around him go as well? Or are they simply left behind, singed and burned?

DERRICK FOUND REBECCA HEADING TOWARD ENGLISH CLASS on Monday morning, making their way through the halls of the school, the lockers adorned with paper Christmas decorations. Along with the talent show at the end of the semester, there was also a contest for the best-decorated locker.

So far, Derrick's was completely bare. He was too busy with the band and tightening up the songs they planned to play for the talent show to focus on the locker competition. AJ's locker, in contrast, was adorned with a paper Christmas tree, the trunk made to look like a guitar neck, with tiny glittering guitars hung from the branches. It was excessive, gaudy, and one hundred percent AJ.

Derrick walked a little faster through the hallway, catching up to Rebecca.

"Hey," he said, coming up beside her.

She turned, though barely acknowledged him.

"I just wanted to apologize for yesterday," he said. "I didn't know that my stepdad, um."

"It's fine," she said. "I didn't know that your stepdad is Officer Reynolds."

"What was that about?" he asked. "Why doesn't Doug like you?"

"I don't want to talk about it, okay?" she sighed.

They walked into their shared classroom just as the tardy bell rang and she sank into her seat, slouching against the plastic back. Derrick wanted to talk to her, to explain that he wanted to be her friend, despite Doug's words. However, she turned away from him and he took his seat next to AJ's.

"What's wrong, bro?" AJ asked, though Derrick waved him off.

Before he could ask another question, Mrs. Rogers began handing out paper packets. "Today we will be studying the balcony scene in Romeo and Juliet. You'll be working in pairs."

Derrick turned to Rebecca as if to invite her to be his partner, but she immediately turned to the girl next to her. He then looked at AJ, who was already scooting his desk close to Derrick's.

"You get to be Juliet," AJ said with a facetious grin.

"Yeah, whatever," Derrick replied as he read over the instructions printed on the pages.

"Dude, what's bothering you?"

Derrick leaned in, glancing quickly toward Rebecca, who was already in mid-conversation with her partner, a nerdy girl named Lyla. In a near-whisper, he said, "It's

Rebecca. Doug doesn't like her for some reason, and I don't know why. When he showed up yesterday, she looked like she was in serious trouble, and he told me she's not welcome at our house. I just don't get it."

"Well, it's probably not her that he has something against," AJ said. "It's probably her mom."

"What's her mom have to do with it?"

"I'll explain at lunch," AJ said. Then, with a hint of hesitation, "Her mom has a bit of a reputation."

It clicked into place for Derrick. Doug had probably arrested her mother in the past. Small towns have a way of making things stick through generations. Working through the Romeo and Juliet assignment, Derrick thought a lot about those Montagues and Capulets and their children, how they got caught in the crossfire of their families.

♪ ♪ ♪

"So that's why she lives with her grandma now." AJ finished the story, taking a bite from his sandwich and washing it down with a swig from the can of Surge.

"That sucks," was all Derrick could get out.

"Yeah. I mean, she's been kind of standoffish ever since the seventh grade. I do think she likes you, though."

"Really?" Derrick asked.

"I mean, I think so. She did come to watch you play yesterday."

"She came to hear the band," Derrick countered.

"No way, man," AJ said. "She was watching you and that's it. Me and Dustin could've been mannequins."

Derrick felt that, too, despite feigning ignorance. Across the cafeteria, he spotted Rebecca sitting alone, writing in a notebook. "I'm gonna go talk to her," he said.

"Good luck," AJ shrugged.

Derrick stood up from the bench and walked to the table at the end of the large cafeteria where Rebecca sat.

"Hey, can I sit with you?" he asked.

She sighed, closing her spiral notebook. "Sure," she capitulated.

He sat on the bench next to her, straddling it. She instinctively leaned away from him.

"Look, I don't know what's gone on in the past with your family, and your mom or whatever. And, really, I don't care. You're cool to me, and I want to be friends with you."

She sat in silence for a moment, and finally said, "That's really sweet, but I don't know if I can hang out with you. I mean, it would just be too awkward."

"It's not awkward at all," he said. "I mean, it wasn't awkward before. Like I said, I don't care what's happened. It's like Romeo and Juliet. Just because our parents don't get along or whatever, doesn't mean that we have to stay away from each other."

"Oh, so we're going to fall in love and then kill ourselves?" she asked.

"What? No, I," Derrick stammered, and then he noticed a slight grin creep across her face. "You're a smartass, you know that?"

All his worries melted. "We have a new practice space for the band," he said. "If you're interested in coming to hear us again."

"That's cool," she said. "Did you guys get shut down for good?"

"Well, we just decided it would be best to find somewhere that we could practice without fear of having the cops called if we got loud. Plus, I'd like for you to hear us again, you know, before the talent show."

"I'd like that," she said.

As they talked, AJ eventually made his way over, inviting himself to sit with them after seeing that the coast was clear. The three of them spent the entire lunch period talking about music and the upcoming talent show.

Engaged in conversation, Derrick turned as the cafeteria doors opened and Haley walked in. Derrick saw her immediately, her radiant beauty undeniable though his heart sank as he took in the rest of the scene. She was with a group of jocks, and Ty was in the middle of them, right next to her.

And they were holding hands.

twenty-one

THE WAREHOUSE WAS UNINSULATED AND THEREFORE ALMOST uncomfortably cold. Despite the space heater that they'd set up close to the corner that they practiced in, Derrick's hands ached playing his guitar. The music echoed through and bounced off the metal building's walls, causing their songs to sound muddied. Nonetheless, Rebecca was there, her jacket pulled tight around her body, sitting on a stool, watching and listening to the band practice. She and Derrick had spent nearly every afternoon together after school, parting ways before Doug got home. The rumors around the school had quickly began to spread and whether they made it official or not, they were an item.

Outside of this practice session, Derrick hadn't even spoken to AJ or Dustin, having spent his lunch periods and after school with Rebecca. Even now, Derrick felt a sort of tension that he didn't acknowledge. It was there, however.

After they finished the song, she spoke loudly over the hum of the amplifiers, "That was really good, but I feel like the bass part overpowered the guitar solo in the bridge," she said.

AJ put his hands on his hips. "That's how we wrote it," he said.

"Well, it could sound better," she quipped.

"Nobody asked you, Rebecca," AJ said defensively.

"Guys, let's just play through the list. We need to make sure these are solid before next weekend," Dustin said.

Derrick just shook his head. "Let's take a little break." He motioned for AJ to follow him outside.

Once outside of the warehouse, under a security light, their breath visible and illuminated in the glow, Derrick said, "Do you not want her here?"

"Not really."

"She doesn't mean to come off as bossy or anything," Derrick said. "She just wants us to sound good for the talent show."

"Well, maybe you should listen to the guys who are actually playing in it with you instead of some girl," AJ said.

"She's not just some girl, man," Derrick countered. "She really cares about the music and our band."

"If she cared so much about the band, she wouldn't try to take so much of your time so that we could actually practice when we're supposed to," AJ said.

"It wasn't her fault I was late, man," Derrick said. It was a lie, though. He didn't want his parents to see him with her, so he had walked to her house first before they'd gone to the warehouse together.

"Look, whatever, Derrick. I thought it would be cool to have her around at first. I thought you guys would be cool.

But it's pretty clear you'd rather spend time with her than with us. We're trying to make this band happen, and you've got your head shoved up her ass."

"That's not fair," Derrick said. "For once in my life, a girl shows some interest in me. Just let me enjoy this."

"It's cold out here," AJ said. "Let's go back in and finish the setlist." He turned to head back in the door, but Derrick stopped him with a hand on his shoulder.

"You were my first friend in this town. You're my best friend. I promise, I'm not letting anything get in the way of this band."

AJ didn't say anything, but held his hand to the door. Finally, he said, "You're my best friend too. I just don't want to lose what we have with this band. We have something special. I really think this could take us somewhere."

"I know," Derrick said. They went back inside to get ready to practice.

Dustin got a message on his beeper and he looked at his waistband. "Guys, gonna have to call it a night after this song. My dad needs me back at home."

"Alright," AJ said. "Let's go through that new one that AJ wrote."

"Are you guys going to play that at the talent show?" Rebecca asked.

"Yeah," AJ said.

"I don't know if that's a good idea. People are going to want to hear songs they know," she said.

"It's a *talent* show, Rebecca," AJ said. "We want to show off our *talent*."

"Right, but I think maybe you'll get more of a response if you—"

She was cut off by Dustin. "We can either argue or we can play. Either way, I'm going to have to go soon."

Derrick nodded and, as Dustin counted off the beat, he played the opening riff to the song. They played it almost flawlessly, getting better each time. Once they finished the song, they quickly put away their gear and rolled up the instrument cords, placing everything tidily into a corner of the warehouse behind the drumkit.

Dustin led them out of the warehouse and back into the cold night air. Though only 8pm, the sun had set nearly two hours prior, allowing the cold to set in. The air felt humid, like snow could be expected to start falling at any moment. Dustin and AJ left together in Dustin's pickup and Derrick followed Rebecca to her car.

Once they were in and she got it started—the engine groaned in protest until it finally turned over—she turned on the heater.

"I know you mean well, but AJ takes a lot of pride in what we're doing," he said, hoping to smooth over any tension.

"Well, he may take a lot of pride in it, but it's pretty clear that you have the majority of the talent in this band. I mean, he's a decent bassist, but your guitar playing is amazing. I just don't want to see you held back."

"I don't think I'm held back," he said. "AJ is an amazing guitarist. In fact, he's been playing longer than me, but chose to play bass for the band. He opened it up so that I could play guitar because that's my strong suit."

"Well, I just think that you shouldn't let yourself stay tied to this when you could really go places on your own. Like, after we graduate, you could move to Austin or Nashville and really make it," she said.

"I don't know," he said, but he trailed off. Maybe she was right. Maybe his ticket out of this small town life was moving somewhere that was meant for musicians. He thought about Ben and how his life had stalled here in Mount Vernon. Perhaps this town was meant just as a stepping stone to something bigger, if was able to take the chance.

"You're an amazing musician, and I just don't want to see you get stuck here in a small town," Rebecca said, as if she could read his mind.

"What about you?" he asked. "What do you want to do, after graduation?"

"I don't know. I want to get out of Mount Vernon, that much is for sure. I've thought Seattle, or Portland, or just somewhere where I can pursue my art."

"What about an art school?" he asked.

"Art schools are for wannabes," Rebecca scoffed. "I want to be in it. On the streets, with the real artists. Like in Seattle, there's this huge art scene. All these punk rock zines come out of there, and I just want to be a part of that."

"Have you ever been to Seattle?"

"No," she said. "But it's all there, just waiting for me." Then, she turned to him. "We should go together."

He stammered, but she reached out and took his hand.

"I'm serious," she said. "Let's get out of this town

together. We can move to Seattle. You can pursue your music, and I can be an artist. It would be perfect."

He didn't know how to answer. It was a ludicrous idea, but it spoke to him. In a way, he'd been waiting for someone like Rebecca to come along, to encourage him in this pursuit. Sure, it sounded crazy, but most great ideas do. They could find the music scene in Seattle, and make art and music, leaving everything holding them back behind.

AJ wanted to play a school talent show and make a demo tape. It seemed small in comparison to these plans, this idea.

As the thoughts swirled through his mind, he noticed Rebecca inching closer to him in the seat. Her face was inches from his own and he could smell a hint of nicotine on her breath.

He was about to say yes, to start planning their getaway. As she leaned in to him, painfully slow, her lips making their way toward his, Derrick cocked his head to accept her kiss, but it never came.

Flashing lights illuminated the car and she jumped back. The whoop of a police siren echoed through the empty parking lot, and Derrick saw the police SUV behind him. His hands went cold and clammy. He knew he was in trouble.

There was a rap on the driver's window and Rebecca rolled it down. Doug stood outside the car and leaned into the open vehicle, the rush of warmth spilling out.

"Time to go home, Ms. Winters," he said curtly. "Derrick, get out of the car and come with me."

Rebecca said, "Yes, sir," and gave Derrick an apologetic look.

He was not apologetic. He was angry. He got out of the car and stomped to Doug's SUV and got in the passenger seat.

Doug got in and they watched as Rebecca pulled out of the parking lot. The silence between them was palpable.

Finally, as Doug put the vehicle in drive, he said, "What did I tell you about her?"

"You said she wasn't welcome at our home," Derrick said, staring out the window.

"Well, you definitely understand the letter of the law," Doug said sarcastically. "There are some people in this town that I don't want you associating with."

"Why? Why Rebecca? Because she dresses different? Because she's not a cookie-cutter goodie-two-shoes girl like Haley next door? She understands me. She gets what I'm trying to do with my life."

"You're fifteen years old. You don't know what you want to do with your life," Doug said.

"Oh, but you do?"

Doug pulled into the empty parking lot of a gas station and hit the brakes. "Look at me," he said, turning to face Derrick. "I may not be your father, but that doesn't mean I don't care about you. I've seen dozens of guys just like you fail at life because they chose to associate with the wrong people. But, I've also seen guys with a ton of talent who have made it far in life. I get that you're young, but the people you choose to put in your life now affect you for the rest of your life."

"But Rebecca's not a bad person, Doug," he said.

"Son, Rebecca Winters comes from a bad family. I don't

have enough fingers to count how many times I've been called out to her mom's place. Drugs, alcohol, you name it. Rebecca may grow and leave that environment, but for now, she's not someone I want you hanging around." He paused, and Derrick could actually see the man's chin trembling. "Your mother and you kids are the only family I've ever had. I don't want to see you go down a bad path."

Derrick stayed silent for a moment. "Why did you never get married before?"

"I got close, once. When I was a young man. I had just returned from Saudi Arabia, and met a girl. We fell in love. But, she wanted kids." He paused. "I can't make babies."

Derrick's head fell. "I didn't know that."

"It's okay. I accepted it a long time ago. But, I've got you guys now, and your mom and you kids are the best thing that's ever happened in my life," Doug said.

Doug put the vehicle in drive and they made their way back home. Derrick felt like he'd disappointed his new step-dad, and learning of his past experiences made it even more difficult. He kept his gaze out the passenger window the drive home, quiet and still. There was a part of him that understood what Doug had said. But, there was that part of the back of his brain that ached for the things that Rebecca wanted. To run away, to start a new life and to pursue their dreams.

"Hey," Derrick said, breaking the silence. "What was your dad like?"

Doug exhaled sharply. "He was a hard ass," he said. "He was already an old man by the time I was born. I didn't see him much. My mom died the year before I joined the Army. He didn't last much longer after that."

"I'm sorry," Derrick muttered. "I didn't know."

Turning onto Sixteenth from Main Street, Doug nodded. "It's okay. It's probably why I am so protective of your mom and you kids. I never thought I'd have a family again."

Derrick understood now, understood how his mom and his sister and he were what Doug had always been wanting.

"What happened in Djibouti?"

Doug's face whipped around, his eyebrows raised in bewilderment. "What did Evan tell you?"

"He just said to ask you about Djibouti," Derrick shrugged.

Doug laughed, first quiet and subdued and then full-on. "Oh man. Djibouti. I'll tell you this—you get best friends once in your life. Cherish them."

"But you just said…" Derrick trailed off.

"You're a good kid," Doug said. "I'm lucky to have you in my life, but you'll be graduating in just a few years and out on your own. We'll always be here to support you, but your true friends will be the ones who walk through the fire with you. Choose those people carefully."

twenty-two

Doug didn't say anything to his mother about finding Derrick with Rebecca, at least not in front of him. They walked in through the garage and into the kitchen where Dee and Cassandra were already sitting at the kitchen bar top, awaiting their arrival to start eating dinner. A pizza, fresh from the oven, sat on the counter, sliced, with steam rising from the surface.

Doug kissed Dee on the forehead. "Figured I'd give him a ride home from their band practice, seeing as it's so cold outside," he said.

"How was Gary?" she asked.

"He's freaking out about Y2K, even though I told him that he's more than safe. Says he thinks his office computers are already crashing on him," he said with an eye roll. He lifted a slice of pizza from the pan and onto a plate and took a bite.

"Are the computers actually going to crash? Like, it's all going to just stop working?" Cassandra asked between bites.

"I don't know, babe," Doug said. "I would like to think that the guys that designed and built all this computer stuff were smart enough to either fix it or make sure that they won't crash just because of some date change." As he spoke, he scarfed down the pizza.

Derrick took a couple of slices for himself onto a paper plate. "I'm gonna head to my room," he said.

His mother started to protest, but Doug said, "He said he's got a lot to work on tonight before school tomorrow." He gave Derrick a knowing wink.

Derrick nodded and, excused, took his plate to his bedroom. On his bed, he sat with his plate and ate in the quiet. He grabbed his Walkman and headphones and shoved them into the pocket of his jacket. He needed some alone time, and the best place for it was the roof, overlooking the neighborhood. It may be cold outside, but with no wind, it wouldn't bite through his jacket. At the last second, he decided to also grab one of the fleece blankets that lived on his bed, throwing it over his shoulder.

With the rest of the family finishing up dinner in the kitchen, their laughter and conversation audible from the hall, Derrick went to the back door of the second living area, and out to the patio. He hoisted himself up on the roof from the shed and wrapped the fleece around his shoulders as he sat on the shingles.

Derrick nearly placed the headphones over his ears to drown out the world around him when he heard a noise in the yard below. He steadied himself, silent and listened.

From the backyard of the house next to theirs, he could make out the sound of someone sobbing. He quietly inched his way across the roof to look down into the neighboring backyard. Haley was standing in the dark, leaning against one of the posts that supported the patio roof.

"Hey," he whispered.

She jumped, startled, and looked for the source of the voice.

"Up here. It's me, Derrick," he said.

"Leave me alone," Haley said through sobs.

"Are you okay?" he asked.

"No." The answer was curt and annoyed.

"Is it Ty?" he asked.

"I said leave me alone."

"Fine," he said. He started back to the place where he was sitting, where he'd left his Walkman, when she stopped him.

"Wait."

Derrick stopped, and watched as the girl scaled the wooden privacy fence that separated their lawns and helped her as she heaved herself onto the shed and to the top of the house.

The sky above them was heavy with clouds, and it felt like snow was imminent. The lights from the neighborhood shined on the low cloud cover, illuminating the night air in a soft glow. Derrick could see Haley's face was swollen with tears, her eyes red and puffy.

"Sorry I was rude," she said. "I just…"

"It's okay," he said. "Rough night?"

They sat on the shingles, and Derrick wrapped the fleece around her shoulders. Their breath poured into the night air. They sat in the quiet, neither saying a word for several minutes.

"It's my parents," she finally said.

"Yeah?"

"My dad. He," her voice was shaking again, her chin trembling. She took a deep breath and exhaled and continued, "has been having an affair with some woman. I think they're getting a divorce."

The only thing that came from Derrick's mouth was an unbelieving, "Whoa."

He didn't understand it. These families in this neighborhood, with their opulent homes and perfectly manicured lawns seemed to have it all. It was the idea of suburban perfection, like living in a Sears catalogue.

Finally, he said, "I'm so sorry."

"I just needed to get out of the house for a minute," she said. "And Christmas is just three weeks away." She started bawling again, and Derrick leaned into her. She buried her face into his shoulder. A part of him was confused by this, not knowing how to comfort the girl. The other part of him was selfishly glad that it was his shoulder and not Ty Anderson's that she was crying into.

"I remember my parents' divorce," he said as he stared into the clouds. "I'd never heard a woman cry before."

Haley wiped her face with the back of her hands and straightened up, taking her head from his shoulder.

Derrick continued. "I was in kindergarten. I woke up in the middle of the night and heard my mom and dad arguing. I must have gone back to sleep, but when I woke up again, I heard this sound in the kitchen. It was like a dying animal. I got up from my bed and saw my mom in there. We had this little black-and-white tv in there on the counter, and she was watching the news and smoking cigarettes. She looked like she'd been crying all night. She wiped her eyes and said to me, 'Your daddy is gone and I don't think he's coming back.' I don't think she knew what to do with herself."

"Oh my god," she said. "Did he really leave, just like that?"

"Yeah." Derrick nodded slowly. He'd never talked to anyone about that night before, not even AJ. It was a part of his childhood that he'd tucked away in some corner recess of his brain.

"I don't get that, how someone could just leave their whole family like that."

"I guess he just didn't want to be a dad anymore. My mom says she thinks he went to Arizona, but who knows. I haven't seen my real father in nine years," he said. He turned to her and he could tell she was on the verge of breaking down again.

"I'm sorry. I didn't mean to make you more sad. I guess what I'm saying is, I wish I was older when it happened. I wish I could have understood what happened between them. For me, my dad was there one day and gone the next," he said.

"I just don't understand why he'd do this to us," she said. "My parents always seemed like the perfect couple. High school sweethearts."

"Maybe the things we want in high school aren't what we need when we grow up," Derrick said.

"What's that supposed to mean?" she asked indignantly.

He just shrugged. "Just, maybe the things we think we

want when we are teenagers don't line up with who we grow up to be."

"But this isn't just choosing a different job or not liking the same music. This is family. Kids and parents and everything," she said. "How can you just choose to love someone and then change your mind?"

"I don't know," Derrick said. "But, I don't think you can expect to be the same person twenty years from now. Life changes you." A snowflake flitted from the sky and landed on the blanket in front of them. "Maybe I'm not even making sense."

"What do you want?" she asked.

"I know I don't want to be stuck in a small town like this for the rest of my life," he said. "What about you? What do you *really* want in life?" He recalled one of their first conversations, sitting at the tennis courts, Haley talking about growing up to take over their family business.

"You can't laugh," she said, semi-serious.

Derrick crossed his heart. "No laughing. I swear."

"I want to go to L.A. or New York and be a fashion designer," Haley said. "But at the same time..." she trailed off. "I don't know."

"No, tell me," Derrick said.

"It's just, maybe I really am meant to be like my parents. Live in Mount Vernon for the rest of my life. Raise some kids, take over the family business. Maybe for some people, that's all there is."

More snowflakes fell from the cloud, first a couple and then in dozens.

Derrick held his knees to his chest. "I think a lot of

people have big dreams, but who actually grows up to make them happen? Like, will I actually be a rockstar?"

"I think you can do whatever you set your heart to," she answered.

When she spoke, her eyes held onto his own. Derrick slid his hand over and interlaced her fingers in his. Her hand felt warm in the cold winter air. He didn't want to let go, ever.

"We'd better get down before we're stuck up here," she said.

"I think you're right," he said, releasing his grip from her hand. "Are you going to be okay?"

"Honestly? Probably not. But this made it a little better," she said. "Thank you for talking with me."

"I guess I'll see you at school in the morning." Derrick went to stand and helped Haley up as well.

"Do me a favor and don't mention this to Ty, please," she said.

He wanted to ask her why she was with him, why she chose to date someone like Ty Anderson. He wanted to tell her that he was holding her back. That what she wanted now would just end up in heartbreak when she was older. Instead, he gave her a half-smile. "Of course. We're just friends."

"You're a sweet guy, Derrick," she said as they walked to the ledge of the roof. "You're going to be something someday."

"Maybe," he said. "If we live that long."

"What does that mean?"

"I don't know. I was just thinking about all this Y2K

stuff. My stepdad had to go calm someone down earlier. People are already freaking out."

What color was in the girl's cheeks drained, and Derrick shook his head. "I'm sorry. It was nothing, and he's sure that everything is going to be okay. I shouldn't have said anything."

"Maybe the end of the world wouldn't be such a bad thing," Haley said with a sigh. Derrick held her hand as she shimmied down onto the shed and then to the grass below. Derrick followed.

"Maybe you're right," he said, as his feet plopped onto the crunch of dead grass. The ground was already glistening with moisture, ice forming on the dormant yellowed grass. He watched as Haley went back to her house.

Derrick couldn't help but think that the end of the world would probably fix a lot of problems.

twenty-three
♫ U2 – ONE ♫

IT WAS THE LAST DAY OF SCHOOL OF THE SEMESTER, AND THE hallways were rowdy with excitement for the talent show that evening. AJ found Derrick on the way to their English class and waved him down, a sheet of paper held high above his head.

"I got it!" he said.

Derrick slowed and waited for his friend to catch up to him.

"I got the schedule," AJ said, holding the sheet to Derrick. Taking it from AJ, Derrick perused the itinerary. Of the groups and students who applied for a spot in the talent show, only six were accepted. Stealth was listed as the fourth spot, just after a group of girls doing a dance routine.

Mr. Greene, the band director, was kind enough to let Dustin, Derrick and AJ store their instruments and gear in a storage closet in the band hall. They'd gone to the warehouse and packed all the equipment early this morning before school.

"This is crazy. We're the only band in the talent show," Derrick said.

"We're the only band in the whole school," AJ shrugged. "Which means we have the upper hand here. Nobody else is going to be doing what we're doing up there."

Derrick saw his point. "Hey, have you seen Haley this morning?" he asked.

"No, why?"

"She wasn't in Biology class, and I just wanted to know if she's okay," Derrick said as they walked into the classroom together.

"Why wouldn't she be?"

Sitting in their desks, Derrick leaned across the aisle. "She came over last night," he whispered. "It's her parents. They're getting a divorce apparently," he said.

AJ nearly did a double-take. "Are you serious? Why? Her parents are, like, Mount Vernon's first couple."

"I'll tell you later," Derrick said. Behind them, Rebecca came into the classroom just as the tardy bell rang. She averted her eyes from Derrick's, taking her seat quickly. Though he tried to get her attention, she paid no attention to him.

He wanted to talk to her, to let her know that everything was okay between them, despite what happened with Doug. He knew she was probably embarrassed, but to treat him like he didn't even exist made him upset, like he'd done something wrong.

Before he could talk to her, though, Mrs. Rogers walked in, lugging a television cart. "Last day of the semester, so we are going to watch the movie adaptation of Romeo and Juli-et," she announced to a mix of groans and *ooh*'s.

Derrick looked at AJ, who pulled out his notebook to scrawl on a page of lyrics he was working on. He'd been busy reworking some of the lyrics for the songs they planned on recording for their demo tape, his notebook covered in scribbles and notes scrawled in his messy hand-writing. On the weekend nights that they spent the night at each other's houses, they went over the songs over and over, tweaking them until they were perfect. However, Derrick was convinced that they were never really done. Eventually they'd be set on tape, no longer able to be edited or changed.

As Mrs. Rogers prepared the video cassette on the cart, Derrick ripped a sheet of paper from a spiral notebook and wrote a note on it.

Are you mad at me?

He folded the sheet and, with Mrs. Rogers busy fumbling with the controls on the front of the VCR, turned and handed the note to Rebecca. She took it with a sigh.

After a few moments, with the television playing and the lights turned down low, Derrick felt a tap on his shoulder and he reached around without turning, holding his open palm behind his back. Rebecca placed the note in his hand and he clasped it. In the glow of the television screen, he read her reply.

No. I just don't think we should be friends.

Beneath her words, he wrote out his response.

We can still be friends.

He held the folded paper behind his back and felt her take it from him.

After a few seconds, her felt the tap on his back again, and he once more held his open hand behind him. He felt her place the paper there, her fingers lingering on his for a heartbeat, filling his chest with warmth. With the page in their shared grasp, he held onto her hand for a few moments more before she pulled away.

He unfolded the page again, and underneath his words were hers.

Good luck tonight.

♪ ♪ ♪

WHAT SNOW HAD FALLEN EARLIER IN THE WEEK HAD MOSTLY melted, piles of gray slush still hanging on in the recesses of buildings and shadows. The walk home after school was cold and Derrick pulled his coat tightly around him as he started on his way toward his neighborhood. He knew the next few hours would go slowly, just as the entire day had. Even as he crossed the street, he could see movement and action already at the school's auditorium as preparations for the talent show were underway.

Despite AJ's excitement about the schedule of the night's events, Derrick felt more apprehensive than ever. The pressure of performing in front of the entire school was getting to him, and practicing and rehearsing were starting to feel like work instead of having fun.

"Hey!" he heard AJ's voice behind him.

Derrick slowed to wait for AJ as he jogged up. "Hey man, I didn't see you much today. Are you ready for tonight?"

"I guess. As ready as I'll ever be," Derrick answered curtly.

"Oh come on, Derrick. What's wrong?" AJ asked.

"I'm just burned out on all this," Derrick admitted. "On all the rehearsing, playing the same songs over and over. I'm glad the talent show is tonight because I don't know how much more of this I can take."

"Is this about Wednesday night? With Rebecca?"

"Sort of. Some of it. I don't know. I just miss jamming being fun, and it hasn't been fun for me in a long time. I don't know why. It feels like work."

AJ didn't respond, just looked at his shoes as they continued walking.

Derrick continued, "I don't think it's your fault, or her fault, or anyone's, really. It just feels like we have spent so much time preparing for this talent show that we have forgotten *why* we wanted to do it in the first place."

"I understand that, but we have a good thing here, Derrick," AJ said. "You're not just the most talented musician I've ever met, but you're also my best friend. I don't want you to think this is work. I want to be a musician so that we can make music and enjoy life for the rest of our lives."

"I want that, too. But right now it just feels like it's too much. I think maybe after the show tonight I'd like to take some time away from rehearsing."

"But what about the demo tape?" AJ asked.

"We can work on it after Christmas," Derrick said. "I just want some time to unwind. There's so much going on that I haven't really taken the time to slow down."

"Is this about Haley's parents?" AJ asked.

"Partly, if I had to be honest," Derrick shrugged. "It's that, it's Rebecca, it's this whole music thing in general. Like, what if we're not destined to 'make it'? There are so many musicians who never leave their own town, who never play in front of an audience. What makes us special?"

"What makes us special?" AJ said incredulously. "You, man! You're the heart of this thing. We live and die with you."

Though he was sure that AJ meant well, the prospect of being the main component of their band didn't sit well on his shoulders.

They had almost made it to Derrick's house, and AJ continued, "For me, this band, our music, it's what lets me drown out everything else around us. All I know is, when we're making music together, when we're jamming out and I can feel Dustin's bass drum in my chest, it's all I ever dreamed of."

"Yeah," was all Derrick could muster.

"Look, let's just get through tonight, and then we'll take a break til after Christmas," AJ said. "We can record after Christmas when I get my four-track."

They walked up the sidewalk to Derrick's house and walked into the warm and inviting living room. Doug was home for the day, and he was stoking a fire in the fireplace in the living room, squatting in front of it. The whole house had been decorated in Christmas colors, with a wreath hanging above the mantle.

"Hey guys," Doug said, turning to them. "Why didn't you tell me you were walking? I would have come to give you a ride."

"It's okay," Derrick said as he shed his coat and backpack. "I just wanted a few minutes of peace before tonight."

"You boys ready for the talent show?"

"I think so."

AJ nodded. "Yes, sir."

Doug chuckled. "It's okay. I appreciate the respect, but I'm not in uniform. You can just call me Doug."

"Yes sir, Doug," AJ said.

Derrick shook his head and AJ snorted his laughter.

"Well, you guys are going to kill it tonight. I'm excited to hear you play," he said.

"When's mom coming home?" Derrick asked. He and AJ had crossed into the kitchen, sticking their heads in the French doors of the refrigerator.

"Any minute now. We're going to make dinner before going to the auditorium. Tacos tonight," Doug said.

"I like tacos," AJ said.

"Well, you're in luck because Dee's tacos are the best."

As they talked, Derrick looked at the clock. The next three hours could not go fast enough.

twenty-four

THE SCHOOL'S AUDITORIUM WAS PACKED, THE FAMILIES OF THE students spilling in out of the mid-December cold. The large theatre sat nearly a thousand people, with three sections of seating separated by two paths, plus a balcony on the second level overlooking the main level. At the front of the hall, the stage was framed in burgundy curtains that hung in rippling waves of heavy fabric. In the center, a large Mount Vernon Lion was painted on the middle curtain.

The talent show was the Mount Vernon High PTA's biggest fundraiser every year, with the proceeds going toward the senior class end-of-year celebration. Looking at the gathering audience, Derrick thought all of Mount Vernon came out for it. The only time he'd seen so many people from the town in one place was at the football games in the fall.

The groups that were preparing to perform were all seated at the front of the auditorium. While one group was performing, the next would be waiting in the wings backstage. Even as everything was being prepared, his hands were already clammy. AJ, however, looked perfectly calm and relaxed.

"Are you not nervous?" Derrick asked him.

"Not at all. This is awesome. Look at how many people are here. Every single one of these people here is a potential fan. We just have to win them over."

"How are we going to do that?" Derrick asked.

"Rock their faces off," AJ said with a smile.

Dustin appeared from behind one of the curtains on stage and joined them in their seats. "The drums are all set up. All we have to do is drag the riser in place on stage. Mr. Greene is handling the mixing board, and he's got all the microphones hooked up." He grinned. "We're actually doing this."

They were all dressed in matching outfits, Dustin's idea. In black shirts, blue jeans and black Converse sneakers, he'd convinced both Derrick and AJ that it would make the older crowd call to mind The Beatles and The Rolling Stones, the bands in the sixties that revolutionized rock and roll.

"The crowd will love it, I promise," Dustin had told them. So, they obliged, and they stood at the edge of the row of seats.

"Just think," AJ said. "This could be the last time we ever come to this school. Once all the computers go down, the whole world could end up in chaos."

"That's not going to happen," Dustin said. "My dad said that some guy from corporate said the whole Y2K thing is a bunch of bullshit. Just something the news is throwing on TV every night for ratings."

"Well, I hope he's right," AJ shrugged. "Otherwise, it's sayonara."

"Don't say that, man," Derrick said. "I'm already freaking out as it is."

"We're gonna do great," AJ said. He gave Derrick a playful punch to the shoulder.

"We've never played for an audience like this," Derrick said, scanning the gathering crowd.

"Get used to it, because they're only going to get bigger," AJ said.

Right at 7:00pm, the lights dimmed in the auditorium and Mr. Greene walked on stage to a raucous applause.

"Good evening everyone and welcome to the thirty-fifth annual Mount Vernon High School Talent Show," he said. "This year, we have some wonderful performers, and you will be incredibly entertained over the next hour. Before we begin, I would like to hand the microphone over to the PTA president, Molly Wilkins."

Again, a large round of applause, as Mrs. Wilkins crossed the stage. She wore a green dress with red accents, perfect for Christmas. She spoke into the microphone, her voice energetic and lively, full of a youthful exuberance despite being just over forty. "On behalf of the entire PTA, I just want to thank you for coming out and supporting this fundraiser event. I am happy to announce that this year's ticket sales are the highest we've ever seen! This is the largest crowd for the talent show ever!"

The thunderous applause again filled the room, and Derrick gulped. He felt sweat under his armpits and in his hairline. The room felt stuffy all of a sudden, like someone had cranked the heat.

"I'm going to run outside for a second, get some fresh air," he said to AJ and Dustin.

"Want me to come with?" AJ asked.

"No, I'll be right back. I just need to cool off."

Derrick left the aisle and, shouldering past the gathering audience, walked up the ramp to the foyer and outside. The cold air wasn't as bitter as it was calming. The sky had that same look as it had that night that it started snowing, the clouds pregnant with impending precipitation.

He walked off the sidewalk away from the front doors and to one of the benches that populated the walkway between the school and the auditorium building. As he started up the sidewalk, he saw Haley and her mother coming toward the auditorium. Ducking out of the way, toward a bench in the shadow of a tree, he knew he'd been spotted.

Out of the corner of his eye, he saw Haley break away from her mother and come up to him under the tree.

"Are you hiding?" she asked.

"Why weren't you at school today?" he countered.

"I just...couldn't," she looked at the ground, and he could tell that her face was puffy still, the remnants of tears cried in her swollen eyelids.

"I was afraid you weren't going to make it tonight," he said.

"There's no way we were going to miss this. My mom wanted to get out of the house. Though she's worried about people talking, I told her it would be good to be seen."

"I'm glad you're here," Derrick said. His heartbeat was slowing, and he felt calmed.

"I'm glad I get to see your band. I'm excited," she said.

He looked up and she gave him a slight smile, her lips curving up her colorful cheeks.

"Um," he stammered, "where's Ty?"

"I don't know. He's not talking to me anymore."

"Did you guys break up again?" Derrick asked. Last time he'd seen them together, they were holding hands, though that had been nearly two weeks ago.

"I…" she trailed off. "I don't know. I feel like I've been hanging onto a Ty that doesn't exist anymore. And even though I have tried to forgive him and move on, I just can't get over what he did at my pool party. And then the way he beat up your friend. It's just…he's different now."

"I understand." His own relationship with Rebecca was up in the air as well.

"Listen, I wanted to tell you first, before I told anyone else. I'm not coming back next semester." Her eyes stayed on the ground, averted from his.

Derrick felt a lump in his throat.

"Why?" he started, though she cut him off.

"My mom and I are moving across town, to an apartment. I'm going to Prep next semester."

Derrick pursed his lips.

From the doorway of the auditorium, Derrick saw AJ appear, searching for him. AJ, seeing Derrick on the bench, waved him over and then went back inside the shelter and heat of the building.

"I'd better go," he said. "Looks like we're about to get started."

As he walked toward the auditorium, Haley called out his name, and Derrick turned back around to her.

"I just wanted to tell you that I'm proud of you," she said.

She walked toward the entrance of the building, making her way to the gathering crowd that filed in through the main doors that led inside as Derrick stood silently, taking in her words. After a few moments, he made his way across the school's lawn and toward the auditorium's back door to the stage area, lost in his thoughts.

Haley and Rebecca, his friends, and their band. This entire semester had been a whirlwind, but Doug's words stood out among everything.

Your best friends walk with you through the fire. Derrick's heart beat fast in his chest, knowing that he was about to go on stage with his best friends.

A hand grabbed his collar and jerked him back away from the building.

He was shoved to the ground and before he realized what was going on, he was surrounded by a group of at least four guys.

Derrick immediately recognized them from the football team.

"Alright, asshole," Ty said, emerging from the shadows.

Derrick's eyes went wide. He felt the cold wetness of the snowy grass beneath his body and he couldn't get any traction to get away. Even if he could, he knew he was completely surrounded.

He also knew that, here on the backside of the auditorium building, unless someone came out of the stage door, no one could see them. He was trapped.

Ty continued, "I've had it with you. Ever since you came to school here, you've been a pain in my ass. Every time I turn around, you're talking to my girlfriend. It ends tonight." He turned to one of his friends. "Did you get it?"

One of the other football players, shorter than the rest, but built like a barrel, came toward Ty. "Yeah," he said. "It was backstage with the rest of the stuff."

The kid handed Ty a guitar.

Derrick's guitar.

Derrick tried to stand up but he was shoved back down to the ground. Tears immediately welled in his eyes.

"Please," he begged. "I'm sorry. But don't break my guitar. I need that."

Ty paid no attention to him, however. Lifting the instrument high above his head, he brought it down to the ground. The wood splintered against the concrete walkway, thudding hard as the neck snapped.

Derrick screamed obscenities, crying and spitting.

"No!" he continued to yell.

"Now we're even. You took Haley, I took your stupid guitar."

A man's voice from the sidewalk called out. "Hey!"

The football players looked toward the source as the man started jogging toward them.

"What the hell is going on over here?" the guy asked.

The football players scattered, sprinting away, leaving Derrick sobbing in the snow-covered grass.

Derrick cradled his guitar in his hands, the maple neck

snapped at the twelfth fret. The headstock fell lazily against his lap, held by the strings.

The man knelt next to him.

Derrick looked up.

It was Ben.

"What the hell happened?" And then, taking in the guitar, said, "Oh no."

"Those football players. Ty," Derrick tried to explain through his sobs.

There was no way he could play in the talent show now. Even if he could get AJ's guitar from his house, they didn't have enough time.

"Wait. What are you doing here?" Derrick asked, wiping the tears from his cheeks.

"I help Mr. Greene run sound for the talent show every year, make a little bit of extra Christmas money," Ben said.

"I can't play now," Derrick said, lifting the shattered guitar. "They broke it."

"Get up," Ben said. "I've got an idea."

Holding the remnants of a cigarette in between his fingers, he flicked the butt to the ground and helped Derrick to his feet. Derrick grabbed the Telecaster, examining the damage. The body was cracked and the neck bent, threatening to snap from the tension of the strings. He fell in lockstep with Ben as they walked to the parking lot, his thoughts raging in his head. It's like those football players were just waiting for him out there, waiting to pounce on him. Had they watched and listened to that entire conversation between Haley and himself?

Opening the trunk of his red Geo Metro, Ben grabbed a

black molded guitar case, pulling Derrick's attention back to the moment.

"Use mine," he said.

Derrick looked at him, stunned.

"Meeting you, talking about music with you, it really made me want to play again. I realized that I missed it. I still have this old guitar and I got it set up at Sherman's over the weekend," Ben said.

Setting the guitar case on the hood of the vehicle, he flicked the clasps and opened it up.

Inside, cradled against the black velvet interior, was a butterscotch blonde Telecaster. Unlike Derrick's shiny red instrument, it was worn and beat up, with paint chipped and rubbed off, exposing the wood grain beneath. The black pickguard was scuffed and scratched, lined etched in the plastic.

Derrick's breath caught in his chest. "It's perfect," he said.

"It's yours," Ben said. "I'll trade you."

Derrick looked at him, unable to process what he'd said. Derrick's guitar was nice, but it was new. Despite the broken neck, it was a four-hundred dollar instrument. You couldn't put a price on the years that Ben's guitar had seen. You couldn't put a price on all the music it had made over those years.

"You can't be serious," Derrick said.

"One hundred percent serious," Ben said as he took Derrick's broken guitar and ran his hands over the red Telecaster's body. "I can fix this." The man examined the neck and the place where it bolted onto the body.

"But I think this guitar," he pointed to the blonde instrument in the case, "is ready for a new master."

Derrick took it in his hands reverently, examining every scratch and paint chip.

"Now get in there," Ben said. "And give 'em hell."

THE LIGHTS ON THE STAGE WERE BLINDINGLY BRIGHT AND THE cheers of the audience were still echoing through the auditorium as the girls left the stage and Derrick, Dustin and AJ pulled their equipment on. They'd had the microphones, amplifiers and guitars all plugged into the mixing board and ready to go while Lindsay Gunther and her friends did a lip-sync dance to Nsync's "Bye Bye Bye."

AJ took a look at Derrick, the butterscotch blonde guitar in his hands.

"What is that?" he asked.

"It's a guitar."

"I mean, I know what it is, but where did you get it?"

"Long story," Derrick said. "I'll tell you after we go on."

Once everything was in place and Derrick had his guitar slung over his shoulder, he gave it a quick strum to ensure it was in tune. It sounded smooth and bright. The worn body of the guitar had a heft to it that was more than just the wood. It was all the experiences the instrument had seen. The pedal at his feet showed a green light with each string and he knew they were ready. He gripped the neck, admiring the worn finish. How many songs had been played on this thing? How many stories did it hold? He would ask Ben to tell him all of them.

The lights went down and Mr. Greene came onto the stage to introduce them.

"For our fourth act tonight, I would like to introduce a rock band called Stealth, made up of Derrick Townsend and AJ Tooley, both sophomores and Dustin Duncan, a junior." He paused for an introductory applause, and then turned to the band. "Ready when you are, boys."

Mr. Greene left the stage, and as the house lights dimmed completely, Derrick looked out to the audience, catching friends and family. He caught a glimpse of Haley, who waved at him with a bright grin on her face, and his parents near the front. His mother had the camcorder in hand, the device strapped to her wrist. Even from the stage, he could see the red LED power light on the front. This performance, no matter how it went, would be forever saved to home video.

He scanned the room for Rebecca, hoping to see her in the sea of people, but she was nowhere to be found. His heart dropped. Even if things hadn't worked out between them, he still wanted her to be here.

Pulling him back from his thoughts, Dustin called out, "Alright, here we go. One, two, three, four." He beat his drumsticks together to the count, the tempo set for Derrick.

As he played the opening riff of the Collective Soul song, his guitar echoing through the auditorium, he had never heard anything so loud, so full. The people in the first few rows began cheering immediately, and Derrick stepped on the wah pedal as they hit the verse.

AJ's voice rang out in the mix, singing the lyrics in a near spot-on Ed Roland impression, breathy and raspy. The monitors placed in front of them that allowed them to hear their mix helped keep them in time, though they'd played the song so many times in rehearsals that Derrick thought they could do it completely isolated from each other and still hit their cues on mark.

It was when he hit the guitar solo in the song that his pulse raced, because when he hit the sweeping arpeggios, the crowd went wild with cheers and shouts. The energy felt like an actual rock concert, which made Derrick play more ferociously.

In that moment, with the auditorium full of people bobbing their heads and moving to the music, with his best friends on stage with him, Derrick knew. No matter what— whether it was in Mount Vernon or far away in the Pacific Northwest, or at some college campus—he wanted to do this for the rest of his life. He wanted to play music, to perform, to write songs and play them in front of huge crowds for as long as he could.

They finished the song to a raucous round of applause. AJ spoke into the microphone, "Thank you, Mount Vernon! We are Stealth. On drums is Dustin Duncan." Dustin played a quick round on the toms. "To my left, the best guitarist in the entire world—Derrick Townsend!" To that, more cheers from the crowd.

Derrick looked out at the audience, finding Haley. She stood on her feet, next to her friends, beaming.

"And I'm AJ Tooley," he continued. Looking down to the table of six judges—various members of the school faculty as well as an honorary judge, a local celebrity who had come back to town for this talent show—he said, "We hope to get your first-place votes. This next song is our last, but one we wrote. My best friend Derrick is going to take it from here."

AJ nodded at Derrick, and he switched his foot pedals connected between his amplifier and guitar to the new tone. The Telecaster in his hands felt like an extension of his body, like an extra appendage and not something separate.

The song was a mid-tempo rocker with a chunky riff that Derrick had written after listening to the *Achtung Baby* tape that AJ had given him at the beginning of the semester. When they hit the bridge of the song, AJ gave Derrick a look. Once they locked eyes, they knew what to do, unspoken yet apparent. When the bridge shifted back to the chorus, with an eight-beat run down the scale, Dustin hit the cymbals while Derrick and AJ jumped into the air simultaneously, both hitting the same note on the down-beat when their feet hit the ground.

They had played these songs before, in front of other students even, but now they weren't simply jamming. They were *performing*.

The audience's response to the synchronous jump was absolutely deafening. They concluded the second song to cheers and chants of "Encore! Encore!"

Derrick's cheeks hurt from smiling and AJ put his arm

around his shoulders. Dustin came up to the other side and they bowed in unison.

Pulling their equipment off the stage, they went outside to cool off and congratulate each other.

"Dude, that was amazing," AJ said, sweat pouring from his brow despite the cold air. "Did you hear that crowd?"

"Dustin, you hit those beats right on cue. That was the best drumming I've ever heard," Derrick said.

"When did you guys come up with that jump thing?" Dustin asked. "That was the coolest thing I think I've ever witnessed in my entire life. That was actual rockstar shit."

"We just came up with it. He looked at me and I knew," Derrick said.

"Okay, where did you get that badass guitar?" AJ asked.

"Ben gave it to me," he said. He told them the entire story of getting jumped by the football team, about Ty smashing his guitar. They stared at him, stunned.

"That's it, then," AJ said. "That's Ty's third strike. He's done for."

Derrick leaned against the cold brick of the auditorium building, the sweat on his forehead now cool. He didn't want to think about Ty or his goons. He was still riding the high from their performance. "I want to do that for the rest of my life," he said. "I want to be a band forever, making music with you guys. This is a dream come true."

His bandmates agreed. He couldn't imagine things ever getting any better.

♪ ♪ ♪

"AND THE WINNER OF THE 1999 MOUNT VERNON HIGH School Annual Talent Show is…" Mr. Greene held the sheet of paper in his hand, the winner written on it and then folded before he got on stage.

The six acts all sat together in those first few rows of the auditorium, each holding their collective breath. Someone leaned into Derrick's ear and whispered, "It's totally going to be you guys. You tore the roof off this place, bro."

Derrick grinned and whispered a thank you over his shoulder. Mr. Greene let the anticipation hang over the audience for as long as he could and he slowly unfolded the paper.

He grinned, and leaned into the microphone. "With four first-place votes: Lindsay Gunther, Georgia Reed, Gabriella Cohn and Sarah Swan with their performance of NSync's 'Bye Bye Bye.'"

There was a loud, high pitched squeal of cheers. Derrick sunk into the wooden seat. He felt as if his heart was ripped out in front of the entire school. He sat and watched as the four girls, jumping up and down with excitement, went on stage to accept their award.

"That should have been us," AJ said to him, under his breath, his chin resting on his forearms on the chair in front of him.

Derrick didn't respond. He didn't have to.

The dream was over.

twenty-six

CHRISTMAS CAME AND WENT, AND HIS BEDROOM WAS FILLED with new guitar equipment. Though initially excited to have a new amplifier, a Vox AC30, and some new effects pedals, Derrick had hardly touched any of it since Christmas morning. It all sat in the corner of his bedroom, mocking him for what could have been. The guitar that Ben gave him resided in its black case, the latches locked.

He spent nearly the entire break lounging around, playing *Goldeneye* on the Nintendo and watching MTV. Cassandra had received a car—a blue beater of a Saturn, but a car nonetheless—and it seemed that the only time she was home during the break was to sleep. On New Year's Eve, he put on his headphones and tried listening to some of the old mixtapes he'd made, but it all sounded stale. Old. Uninspired.

Or, uninspiring.

Outside, winter had hit with full force, keeping them inside most days.

"Why are you so mopey?" Cassandra asked, standing in the doorway to his room. She was applying lipstick and had on a black skirt, looking as if she were getting ready to leave for a party.

He could have told her any number of things. The fact that his band had been robbed of the talent show winnings. That his band hadn't practiced or played since that night. That their plans of recording a demo tape hadn't come to fruition. That school was about to start again, and he had maybe played his guitar five times all break.

That, if he had to be completely honest to himself, he'd never be a rockstar. Just a guy who played guitar.

"Nothing."

"Come on," she pried. "It's New Year's Eve and I'm having a party. The new millennium is happening. You can't go into 2000 being all sad."

"I'm not sad," he said, his hands behind his head on the pillow. He stared up at the ceiling, watching the blades of his fan spin lazily. "I just don't feel like partying."

"Well, all my friends will be here. It might do you some good to hang out with them. They'll all be seniors next year. You'd be way cooler hanging out with them than your lame friends," she said. She smacked her lips together. "Speaking of," she said, "where are your friends?"

"Dustin is in Oklahoma, visiting his dad's family. I haven't heard from AJ," he answered.

"Well, Casey and Tara are coming over at nine. You should come hang out. Watch the ball drop with us."

"Yeah," he said. "Maybe."

Cassandra shut his bedroom door and he stared at the

ceiling in silence. This was the lamest New Year's Eve ever, and he had no desire to hang out with his sister and her friends.

Pulling himself from his bed, he went into the hallway and found the cordless phone on its base. He dialed AJ's number. It rang a few times. Finally, the line clicked and he heard AJ's mom's cigarette-frayed voice. "Hello?" she said.

"Hey Mrs. Tooley. Is AJ home?"

"He is, but he's grounded. He failed Spanish for the semester, so he's not allowed to talk on the phone until school starts."

"So, he can't come to my house for a New Years' party?" he asked, deflated.

"I'm afraid not," she said.

"Okay. Thanks anyways." Derrick hung up the phone and placed it back on the base. He felt somewhat relieved that AJ hadn't been avoiding him or blowing him off altogether. Though any shot he had at having fun tonight was decimated. He wished he had a television in his room so he could watch the ball drop in New York by himself. Something to drown out the silence of his boredom.

Back in his bedroom, he grabbed his acoustic guitar and played a few chords, humming along with it. It was a melancholy sound, minor chords picked note by note. He leaned against the headboard of his bed and strummed along lazily. It didn't sound inspired, but it was something.

From the living room, he could hear girl's voices, shrill and loud, echoing down the hall. Their parents were at a party with the police department, leaving the house to them tonight. He thought about going into the living room to hang out, grab a slice of pizza and watch the celebration on television with them, but he didn't want to make it awkward.

Suddenly, he heard footsteps coming down the hall and Cassandra knocked on the door before opening it a moment later.

"Hey, the girls want you to come and play a song for them," she said.

"I don't want to play a song for them," Derrick said.

"Please," she begged. "They think you're really good, and every party needs a guy with a guitar."

"Ugh," he groaned. "Okay. One song."

He felt lame by himself, so he grabbed his guitar and followed Cassandra to the living room. Her friends saw him and perked up, clapping.

"You were so good at the talent show," Tara said. She was sitting on the couch, her feet curled up beneath her and she cradled a Pepsi in her hands. Her dark hair was kinked tightly and spilled out over her shoulders.

"Seriously," Casey said from the recliner. "You guys got robbed. Lindsey and her friends do the same thing every year, that whole lip sync dance routine. They just do a different song. You guys had actual talent."

"Thanks," Derrick said. He rested his forearm on the body of the guitar. "I only play for tips now, so get your dollar bills ready."

Both girls laughed and Cassandra rolled her eyes.

"Okay, for real, what do you want to hear?" he asked, fiddling with the tuning keys on the headstock.

"Anything," Casey said. "Something upbeat."

Derrick began strumming a few chords and sang along. "It's the end of the world as we know it," he started, and the girls burst out laughing.

"That's not really going to happen though, is it?" Tara asked, her mood quickly serious.

"No," Cassandra said, her response irritated. "It's just a ploy to get people to buy more stuff. Of course the computers aren't going to crash."

But, the idea still held in Derrick's mind. *What if this is the end?*

Derrick told the girls to have a good time, and that he was going up on the roof.

"Oooh," Tara said, "let us know if you can see the fireworks from up there, and we'll come with you."

"Alright," Derrick said, standing from the couch, though he had no intentions of doing so. If this was it, the last night before the world went to hell, he'd spend those last moments alone.

In his bedroom, he deposited his guitar, threw on a jacket and stuffed his Walkman in one of the pockets. A few seconds later, he was outside in the cold winter night, scaling the side of the house from the storage shed and climbing up onto the spot on the roof where he normally sat to listen to music.

As he pulled himself up to the shingles, he froze. Haley was already there.

"Hey," she said, turning to him. "I was hoping you'd come up here soon."

"How long have you been up here?" Derrick asked, still frozen in place.

"Not long. My mom and dad are fighting, and this is the only place I could think of that I could find some solace," she said. She had a blanket pulled across her shoulders, and she motioned for Derrick to join her. "Why aren't you at some party or something?"

"My sister has some friends over, downstairs. I don't know. I don't feel like partying," he answered. He sat next to her as she opened the blanket, letting it envelop him with her. It was already warm.

"I'm sorry," she said. "About the talent show. You guys are really good."

"*Were.*"

"What?"

"Were good. I don't think we're a band anymore," he said.

"Why not?" Haley asked.

"Just," he paused. "Burned out."

"Well, don't stop playing music. I could see the joy on your face when you were on that stage. It made me jealous," she said.

"Jealous?" Derrick gave her a puzzled look.

"Yeah. I don't know anything that gives me that kind of happiness. I have lived my entire life trying to make my parents happy, doing the things they want me to do. Follow the rules, be involved, do extracurricular stuff. And where has that got me?" Haley sighed. "Now, my parents are divorcing and I'm going to a new school and I just wish I had something like that. I wish I had something that made me that happy."

"Music does that for me. It helps me forget all the bad

things around me. I can put on a Pearl Jam or a U2 album and everything just dissolves."

"I never told you, but do you remember that one time we were up here? You gave me that tape. I was being a jerk to you that night, but I listen to that tape all the time," she said.

"Really?" He had assumed that she just shoved it in some errant desk drawer, out of sight. Especially after she and Ty had gotten back together.

"Yeah," she said. "I have it in my stereo in my room. Whenever my parents start going at it and yelling at each other, I turn it on. It's comforting, you know? It helps drown out all the bad stuff."

"I'm glad you like it," he said.

"I heard what Ty did to you. To your guitar."

"It's okay," he said.

"No it's not. And I should have listened to you a long time ago. I should have seen what a jerk he is before I let him hurt me over and over. I have just held hope that he was still the good guy I knew back in middle school. But he's changed. He's awful. Not like you." Her eyes were sad, yet glinting with something that Derrick couldn't quite comprehend. "You're perfect," she said.

She looked at him, and he turned his face toward hers, their eyes and lips dangerously close. A stream of light off in the distance, a few blocks away, shot into the night sky. It was then followed by an explosion of color and a boom.

Haley turned her face away from his and whispered a silent *wow*.

Derrick slid his hand and felt Haley's fingers interlace

with his. It filled him with the same kind of explosion, a bloom of light and color in his whole body.

"It's almost midnight," she said.

"Y2K," he nodded.

"Do you think?" she started.

"I don't know," he said. He knew what she meant though. If this was *the end of the world.* If, in a few moments, life as they knew it would be over. "But if it is, this is exactly where I want to be."

"Me too."

With his free hand, he produced his Walkman and headphones. He pushed play on the device and sound flowed from the earpieces. Leaning close to each other, they held the speakers between them, listening to Bono's voice from the tape as the fireworks shot off in the distance, each one illuminating the dark sky in different colors.

From the houses below, they could hear a collective countdown.

"Five!"

Another firework erupted above them, blossoming in red and purple.

"Four!"

Derrick turned his face to Haley's. Her eyes were bright, the fireworks above them reflecting in her green irises, creating sparkles in the reflection.

"Three!"

She leaned in to him, her hand on the nape of his neck, the sensation sending a tingle down his spine.

"Two!"

He tilted his head and inched his face closer to hers.

"One!"

Their lips touched. Hers soft against his own, he breathed in every ounce of the moment that he could. Electricity flowed through his body and he felt her lips part, her tongue flick at his. Derrick tasted bubblegum as Haley pressed into him.

As the people in their homes below welcomed Y2K, Derrick and Haley welcomed the end of the world with a kiss.

twenty-seven

As it turned out, the world continued spinning on January 1, 2000, and society didn't fall into darkness. The planes in the air stayed their course, the television and radio signals continued to broadcast.

When the second semester started the next week, Derrick was excited to get back to normal and to see his friends. The break had been long and boring. He was ready to get back to the hustle and bustle of school. He missed it.

He hadn't talked to Haley since that night on the roof. They'd kissed, and when the world didn't blow up, she pulled away from his lips and watched the rest of the fireworks show, both in silent understanding. After the encore, dozens of fireworks shooting off in the black sky in near succession, he helped her climb down from the rooftop. They said exchanged goodbyes, and that was it.

In the ensuing days, Derrick watched as a moving truck pulled in front of the Swanson home, and a parade of boxes loaded into the back. He watched from the driveway as she and her mother left, presumably to their new apartment on the other side of town, away from their neighborhood. As their car followed the moving truck and turned the corner out of sight, Derrick stood there, still feeling the buzz of Haley's kiss.

Every night, he thought about her. He sat on the rooftop alone and listened to his tapes. He missed having her so close, having her next door.

This morning, Cassandra drove them to school. Though she was hardly home since getting her car, in a sense, it made them closer. Derrick found himself enjoying the time they did spend together more than they once did. She let him play his music on the stereo, and as they pulled into the parking lot, he thanked her for the ride.

"I'll be here after," she said, a fake grin across her face. "Don't run late. I will leave you."

"Yeah, yeah." Derrick waved her off and pulled his head-phones over his ears, turning up the volume on his Walkman.

Inside the school, just as the first bell rang, Derrick opened his locker and saw something in there already, something that wasn't there when he cleared it out before the break. At the bottom of the shelf, a package had been slipped through the vents. He picked it up, examining the envelope. It was small, wrapped in brown craft paper and tied with a red string, a simple bow looped around it. His name was written on the package in an elegant hand, cursive in black Sharpie.

He pulled the string and unwrapped the package. A tape

spilled out of the wrapping. On the label, in the same hand-writing as on the paper, was scrawled:

Mixtape for the End of the World
Love, Haley

On the back side of the label, he read over the track listing that she'd created. All of his favorite bands were there, and some of her own.

He held the thing in his hands and smiled. He wanted to listen to it immediately, to pop it into the Walkman and drown out the din of school, to transport himself back to that moment on the roof with Haley, that moment that they kissed. Instead he would wait until he was home at the end of the day so he could play it unhindered.

"What's that?" a voice behind him asked.

Derrick pulled the headphones from his ears and hung them around his neck. Turning, he found AJ, standing in the middle of the hallway, a backpack slung lazily over one shoulder.

"Just a mixtape," he said, slipping the cassette case into the back pocket of his Levis.

"Nice," AJ said. "Where's your first class?"

"Mr. Thompson's world geography class," Derrick said.

"Sweet! Me too!" AJ held out his hand for a high five and Derrick hit it with his own. Then, they embraced in a hug.

"I missed you over the break," Derrick said. "Is that weird? I feel like that might be weird."

"Not weird at all," AJ said as they released each other.

"You're the best friend I've ever had. I hated not getting to hang out like we wanted."

They walked to class together in lockstep, right-foot, left-foot, as the students in the hallway filed into their respective first period classes.

"I wrote some new songs over the break," AJ said apprehensively. "And I was thinking about demoing them on my four-track recorder."

"Good," Derrick said. "Let's jam them after school."

"Really?" AJ asked, his face lighting up.

Derrick nodded. "Yeah man," he said. "I'm ready to play again."

♫ THE END ♫

a note from the author

Mixtape is probably the most autobiographical story I've written thus far in my career. Playing in garage bands was a seminal part of my teenage years (yes, we got the cops called on us for a noise complaint), and my biggest goal was to distill those experiences here in way that felt both unique and familiar. I actually started writing this story nearly twenty years ago, while I was still in high school myself, but I could never get it to gel. I don't think I was mature enough as a writer or as a human to do it justice. I'm glad I was finally able to get it out in its current form. It's a story I was meant to tell for a long time.

Music is still so important in my life, and I'm always listening to something, either through headphones or on the record player in our living room at home. Learning to play music, though—learning guitar and piano as a fourteen year-old wayward teenager—was something that gave me some of my best friends and some of the most exciting experiences in high school. If anything, I hope that I distilled those experiences in these 60,000+ words.

As always, there's an entire list of people to thank in these pages.

First and foremost, my wife Jennifer. Thank you for supporting this crazy endeavor. Thank you for coming along to the book signings and the events, always with a smile and a helping hand. And thank you for always letting me choose the soundtrack to our road trips. I love living this life side by side with you.

To the "real" Derrick: When I finally "cracked" this story, I had the realization that I was coming at it from the wrong angle. It wasn't my story that needed to be told—it was yours. I hope I've done it justice. Obviously, I've taken a lot of creative license, but at the heart of it, the story of our friendship and playing music together in a garage band was, and remains, my favorite memory of growing up.

To the indie bookstores that have been so supportive of me and my works: Burrowing Owl Books in Amarillo, TX; Sundog Books in Seaside, FL; Silver Dawn Books in Grand Forks, ND; Ferguson Books in Bismarck, ND; The Book Burrow in Pflugerville, TX—thank you all so very much.

To everyone else, thank you:
    Gabe Morgan
    Andrew Monroe

Derek Tessneer
Lance Adkins
Niccole Caan
Kenny Nagunst
Dusty Boyd
Rick Treon
Danielle Girard
Lyssa Kay Adams
Elizabeth Williams
Rodrigo Godoy
Abby Jimenez
Dallas Bell
Burrowing Owl Books
Jim Livingston
Morgan Duerden

And once again, my most sincere apologies to Derek Porterfield for forgetting to mention you in these acknowledgments pages. I'll make it up to you next time.

Love,

**Listen to the music from
Mixtape for the End of the World here:**

Mixtape for the End of the World Playlist

about the author

Andrew J Brandt is the Pencraft award-winning and bestselling author of multiple novels, including the Reading the West Award nominees *Palo Duro* and *Mixtape for the End of the World*. His 2022 release *Picture Unavailable* spent four weeks as Amazon's #1 new YA release and received a BookFest Award in the YA Category upon publication. In 2023, *Picture Unavailable* was named a finalist for the Silver Falchion Award. Andrew is an on-air contributor for KAMR-NBC4's *Studio 4* program in Amarillo, TX where he hosts a monthly book club segment. His novels have been optioned for television and film. A graduate of West Texas A&M University, Andrew resides in Texas with his wife and children.

Find Andrew online at www.andrewjbrandt.com

www.ingramcontent.com/pod-product-compliance
Lightning Source LLC
Chambersburg PA
CBHW031438200726
48289CB00002BA/631